College English Fast Reading
Students' Guide Book

大学英语快速阅读新导学

（第三册）

总主编：蔡碧霞

本册主编：赵建玲

本册副主编：张秋林

ZHEJIANG UNIVERSITY PRESS
浙江大学出版社

图书在版编目(CIP)数据

　　大学英语快速阅读新导学. 第 3 册/蔡碧霞总主编；
赵建玲分册主编. —杭州：浙江大学出版社，2009.6
　　ISBN 978-7-308-06872-7

　　I. 大…　II. ①蔡…②赵…　III. 英语—阅读教学—
高等学校—教学参考资料　IV. H319.4

　　中国版本图书馆 CIP 数据核字(2009)第 104002 号

大学英语快速阅读新导学(第三册)
蔡碧霞　总主编　赵建玲　本册主编

责任编辑　张　琛
封面设计　卢　涛
出版发行　浙江大学出版社
　　　　　(杭州天目山路 148 号　邮政编码 310028)
　　　　　(网址：http://www.zjupress.com)
排　　版　杭州中大图文设计有限公司
印　　刷　杭州余杭人民印刷有限公司
开　　本　710mm×1000mm　1/16
印　　张　8.5
字　　数　208 千
版 印 次　2009 年 7 月第 1 版　2009 年 7 月第 1 次印刷
书　　号　ISBN 978-7-308-06872-7
定　　价　15.00 元

版权所有　翻印必究　印装差错　负责调换
浙江大学出版社发行部邮购电话　(0571)88925591

前　言

大学英语教学的目的是培养学生具有较强的阅读能力和一定的听说读写译能力，使他们能用英语交流信息。大学英语教学应帮助学生打下扎实的语言基础，掌握良好的语言学习方法，提高文化素养，即具有较强的英语综合应用能力，以适应社会发展和经济发展的需要。教育部颁发的英语教学大纲中，阅读的基本要求(四级)是：能顺利阅读语言难度中等的一般性题材的文章，掌握中心大意以及说明中心大意的事实和细节，并能进行一定的分析、推理和判断，领会作者的观点和态度，阅读速度达到每分钟 70 词。在阅读篇幅较长、难度略低、生词不超过总词数 3%的材料时，能掌握中心大意，抓住主要事实和有关细节，阅读速度达到每分钟 100 词。

阅读理解始终都是各类测试的最重要内容，所占分数比重大。阅读理解既是英语学习和英语测试的重要手段，又是英语学习的终极目的之一。英语阅读是一种创造性的思维劳动，它不仅涉及语音、语法、词语这些最基本的语言要素，而且还包括许多非语言因素，如文化知识背景、思维习惯等。

现有的大学英语教材虽然种类繁多，但能真正帮助学生、针对性较强地解决学生阅读能力的教材却寥寥无几。在多年的教学实践中，我们深深感到，要有的放矢地提高学生的英语阅读能力，必须有相适应的英语阅读教材。其特点必须是由浅入深、体裁广泛、文体多样、趣味性强，既可作教材，在课堂内使用，更重要的是，可由学生在课外自主阅读。阅读量课内外的比例应是 1：4左右。而由于课时原因，阅读不可能全部在课堂内进行，还必须在课外加强。这就要求我们必须给学生准备大量的快速阅读及泛读材料。

鉴于以上种种因素，我们在总结几十年教学经验的基础上，并根据学生的实际情况，殚精竭虑编写了这套《大学英语快速阅读新导学》。其目的就是让学生接触到大量以英语国家为背景的社会、人文、政治、经济、娱乐等方方面面的文字材料，创造出一个模拟的英文环境，在老师的帮助下，拓宽学生的视野。我们的编写原则是强调材料的数量及多样性。

《大学英语快速阅读新导学》共有四册，每册分为 8 个单元，每单元由 4

篇阅读文章组成。文章主要选自当代最新的英文报纸和英文著作,题材广泛,涵盖文化、教育、历史、地理、科技、经济、友情、亲情、校园生活等,并与学生的学习、生活密切相关,是大学生提高词汇量、扩展知识面、培养英语学习兴趣的好帮手。所有文章的内容思想健康,具有知识性、时代性和趣味性,既可提高学生的英语素养,又能增强学生的综合运用能力。每篇阅读文章配有针对性强、形式多样的练习,设有选择题、正误判断、翻译和问答题等题型,以增进英语的习得。所有练习均给出了参考答案。

在培养阅读能力的教学过程中,应在密切关注"快速阅读"的基础上,着重关注以下几个方面:理解文章的主旨和要义,理解文章的具体信息,根据上下文推断生词的词义,根据文章做出简单的推断和推理,理解文章的基本结构,理解作者的意图、观点和态度。另外必须注意的是:相应练习总是以文章为根据,这就是说,答案要在文章中找到根据。因此,我们不仅要求学生注意词汇、语法和阅读理解三大语言要素,掌握一定的语言背景知识,掌握阅读技巧,并有一定的分析和理解能力,同时还希望在注重量的同时注重阅读速度。

阅读是一个循序渐进、厚积薄发的过程,所以这套丛书分为四册,由浅入深,最后达到大学英语四级所要求的词汇量、阅读量和阅读速度。

本册是《大学生英语快速阅读新导学》的第三册。本册的主旨是把握主题,即快速阅读的整体要求。本书要求学生通过寻找文中关键词、要点、事实和细节,推断、判断、归纳、理解文章大意和主旨。提高阅读速度,掌握阅读技巧,增强在句子水平、段落水平及篇章水平上的理解力,进而了解作者意图,并具有一定的鉴赏能力。

本丛书的相关语言问题由英语专家审阅把关,从而保证了质量。

在编写这套书的过程中,尽管我们从主题设计、文章选择、练习设置等方面花了大量的时间和精力,力求使其达成我们理想的教学目的,但由于种种原因,未必能做到尽善尽美。因此,我们衷心希望广大教师和学生在使用过程中不吝指教,以便我们在重印或再版时修正提高。

编　者

2009 春

Contents

目　　　录

Unit 1

Traditional Holidays

> To many holidays are not voyages of discovery, but a ritual of reassurance.
>
> —*Philip Andrew Adams*

Passage 1

Story of Mother's Day

While many people might assume that Mother's Day is a holiday   1
invented by the fine folks, it's not so. The earliest Mother's Day
celebrations can be traced back to the spring celebrations of
ancient Greece in honor of Rhea (瑞亚), the Mother of the Gods.

During the 1600's, England celebrated a day called "Mothering Sunday" (省亲日). Celebrated on the 4th Sunday of Lent (四旬斋) (the 40-day period leading up to Easter Day), "Mothering Sunday" honored the mothers of England.

2

During this time many of the England's poor worked as servants for the wealthy. As most jobs were located far from their homes, the servants would live at the houses of their employers. On "Mothering Sunday" the servants would have the day off and were encouraged to return home and spend the day with their mothers. A special cake, called the "mothering cake", was often brought along to provide a festive touch.

3

As Christianity spread throughout Europe, the celebration changed to honor the "Mother Church"—the spiritual power that gave them life and protected them from harm. Over time the church festival blended with the Mothering Sunday celebration. People began honoring their mothers as well as the church.

4

In the United States, Mother's Day was first suggested in 1872 by Ulia Ward Howe, who wrote the words to the Battle Hymn of the Republic (共和国战歌) as a day dedicated to peace. Ms. Howe would hold organized Mother's Day meetings in Boston every year.

5

In 1907 Ana Jarvis, from Philadelphia, began a campaign to establish a national Mother's Day. Ms. Jarvis persuaded her mother's church in Grafton, West Virginia to celebrate Mother's Day on the second anniversary of her mother's death, the 2nd Sunday of May. By the next year Mother's Day was also celebrated in Philadelphia.

6

Ms. Jarvis and her supporters began to write to ministers,

7

businessmen, and politicians in their quest to establish a national Mother's Day. It was successful as by 1911 Mother's Day was celebrated in almost every state. President Woodrow Wilson, in 1914, made the official announcement proclaiming Mother's Day as a national holiday that was to be held each year on the 2nd Sunday of May.

It is somewhat ironic that after all her efforts, Ana Jarvis ended up growing bitter over the commercialization of the holiday and grew so mad at it that she fielded a lawsuit to stop a 1923 Mother's Day festival. Shortly before her death, Jarvis told a reporter she was sorry she had ever started Mother's Day.   8

Ana may be gone, but Mother's Day lives on. While many countries of the world celebrate their own Mother's Day at different times throughout the year, there are some countries such as Denmark, Finland, Italy, Turkey, Australia, and Belgium which also celebrate Mother's Day on the second Sunday of May.   9

(471 words)

How fast do you read?
   471 words ÷ _____ minutes = _____wpm

Exercises for Passage 1

I. Choose the best answer for each of the following items in accordance with the passage.

1. Based on the knowledge that Easter Day is often observed on the first

Sunday after a full moon on or after 21 March, it is inferred that "Mothering Sunday" might be celebrated in _____.

A. January   B. February   C. March   D. April

2. As far as the history of English Mother's Day is concerned, which of the following is least likely to imply?

A. Mother's Day in England was originally a day of family reunion of poor people.

B. Young people were supposed to buy a special cake for their mothers on that day.

C. With the influence of Christianity, Mother's Day tended to take on a religious color.

D. Nowadays, Mother's Day in England is solely a celebration of church festival.

3. Where did Mother's Day dedicated to peace first appear in the history of USA?

A. In the words of a song.   B. In a declaration.

C. In a passage.   D. In a requesting letter.

4. Why did Ms. Jarvis choose the 2nd Sunday of May as Mother's Day?

A. Because her mother was born on that day.

B. Because that day was her mother's wedding anniversary.

C. Because that day was the second anniversary of the establishment of her mother's church.

D. Because her mother died on that day.

5. As mentioned in this passage, how many countries celebrate Mother's Day on the 2nd Sunday of May?

A. Five.   B. Six.

C. Seven.   D. Eight.

II. Translate the following sentences from the passage into Chinese.

1. The earliest Mother's Day celebrations can be traced back to the spring celebrations of ancient Greece in honor of Rhea (瑞亚), the

Mother of the Gods.

_____

_____

2. A special cake, called the "mothering cake", was often brought along to provide a festive touch.

_____

_____

3. President Woodrow Wilson, in 1914, made the official announcement proclaiming Mother's Day as a national holiday that was to be held each year on the 2nd Sunday of May.

_____

_____

China's Own Valentine's Day

On the evening of the seventh day of the seventh month on the   1
Chinese lunar calendar, looking carefully at the summer sky, you'll
find the Cowherd (a bright star in the west of the Milky Way) and
the Weaving Maid (the star Vega (织女) in the east of the Milky
Way) appear closer together than at any other time of the year.
Chinese believe the stars are lovers who are permitted to meet by
the Queen of Heaven once a year. That day falls on the double
seventh (Qixi in Chinese), which is China's own Valentine's Day.

In Chinese legends, the Cowherd and the Weaving Maid will meet   2
on a bridge of magpies (鹊) across the Milky Way once a year. It's
said that on Chinese Valentine's Day, people would not be able to
see any magpies on that evening because all the magpies have
left to form a bridge in the heavens with their wings. If it rains
heavily on Qixi night, it is because the Weaving Maid is crying
from happiness over meeting her husband on the Milky Way.

Long long ago, there was an honest and kind-hearted fellow   3
named Niu Lang (Cowherd). His parents died when he was a
child. Later he was driven out of his home by his sister-in-law. The
Cowherd was lonely, however, with only the company of that
faithful old ox. He herded cattle and farmed. One day, a fairy from
heaven Zhi Nv (Weaving Maid) fell in love with him and came
down secretly to earth and married him. The Cowherd farmed in
the field and the Weaver Maid wove at home. They lived a happy
life and gave birth to a boy and a girl. Unfortunately, the Queen of
Heaven discovered the Weaving Maid's absence. She was so
annoyed that she had the Weaving Maid brought back to heaven.

The Cowherd was terrified and sad. Then he caught sight of   4
cowhide (牛皮) hanging on a wall. The magical ox had told him
before dying of old age, "Keep my cowhide for emergency use."
Putting the cowhide on, the Cowherd, with his two children, went
after his wife. He was about to reach his wife when the Queen
showed up and pulled off her hairpin to draw a line between the
two. The line became the Silver River in heaven, or the Milky Way.

The Cowherd and the Weaving Maid couldn't meet. The Weaving   5
Maid was so sad and missed her husband so much that the
clouds she weaved seemed sad. Finally, the Queen showed a

little mercy, allowing the couple to meet once every year on the Silver River on the double seventh.

Magpies were moved by their true love and many of them   6
gathered and formed a bridge for the couple to meet on the evening of Qixi.

(465 words)

How fast do you read?
  465 words ÷ _____ minutes = _____ wpm

Exercises for Passage 2

I. Decide whether each of the following statements is true or false. Put "T" for true and "F" for false in the space provided.

_____1. China's own Valentine's Day falls on the evening of the seventh day of the seventh month on calendar.

_____2. It's said that people would not be able to see any magpies because they had all flown to the south on Chinese Valentine's Day.

_____3. The Cowherd was an orphan.

_____4. The God of Heaven drew a line between the Cowherd and the Weaving Maid.

_____5. It was because of the Queen's mercy that the Cowherd and the Weaving Maid could meet once a year on the Silver River.

II. Translate the following sentences from the passage into Chinese.

1. In Chinese legend, the Cowherd and the Weaving Maid will meet on a

bridge of magpies across the Milky Way once a year.

_____

_____

2. Unfortunately, the Queen of Heaven discovered the Weaving Maid's absence. She was so annoyed that she had the Weaving Maid brought back to heaven.

_____

_____

3. Finally, the Queen showed a little mercy, allowing the couple to meet once every year on the Silver River on the double seventh.

_____

_____

$\mathcal{P}$assage 3

"Happy Father's Day, Dad!"

It was Sunday morning. The phone rang. "Is this Gordon Clay?" the operator asked. "Yes," I replied. "You have a long-distance call from your daughter, will you accept?" "Of course," I replied.   1

"Happy Father's Day, Dad!" I heard from the other end. "Thanks, Nat," I said. "Sounds like you have a cold." "This is Jenny," the voice said. I'm confused. "Is this some kind of joke, Nat," I replied, figuring that it was. "No, my name is Jennifer Masters. It's taken me a long time to find you," Jenny continued. "Your name is Gordon Clay, isn't it? You lived in Kansas City, didn't you? You   2 used to go to Barry's Barn dancing, didn't you?" The answers were yes. "Well, do you remember Sharon Masters?" Sharon Masters? I racked my brain, still in somewhat of a fog. "No, I'm sorry I don't," I replied. "You used to dance with her a lot. You even dated her for a while. She's my mother."

What was it saying? I spent a disturbing Sunday working with my   3
dream. The memories started to return. As a teenager, I used to go to the Barry's Barn all the time. There were always a lot of good-looking girls there and, being a good dancer, I got the chance to date many of them.

The pain began to grow within me. "Oh no," I thought. There was   4
a girl I dated for a while. One night she wanted to leave the dance early and talk something to me. I still don't remember much about that evening, but I do remember that she told me she was pregnant. I think I asked if I could help. She said no, that she was going to leave school to have the baby. I remember feeling relieved at the time and subsequently tuned it out of my memory.

In 1994 I decided to give myself a "Father's Day" gift, a plane   5
ticket home to start my search. If she or he didn't want to see me, that's okay. It's just very clear to me how important it was to make the effort to let this person know who his/her natural father is.

I dedicate this story to every man who has ever had sex out of   6
wedlock (婚姻) and to those who didn't get married. And to those who are still willing to create a child by having sex without protection.

I hope you'll join me on this venture and let your child know what   7
kind of a person you've grown up to be! A man in the true sense is

one who is willing to face his own fear and be responsible for all of his actions.

(449 words)

How fast do you read?
   449 words ÷ _____ minutes = _____wpm

Exercises for Passage 3

I. Choose the best answer for each of the following items in accordance with the passage.

1. When the phone rang, _____.
   A. the author was talking with his daughter on another phone
   B. the author was having breakfast
   C. it was Sunday morning, on Father's Day
   D. the author was thinking of happenings in his youth

2. The sentence "I racked my brain" (Line 9, Para. 2) means "_____".
   A. I tried hard to think of something
   B. I remembered something
   C. I thought out something
   D. I forgot something

3. The 3rd paragraph mainly suggests when the author was young, _____.
   A. he was a good dancer
   B. he had many girl friends
   C. he was a person lack of responsibility
   D. he was very naughty

4. The passage mainly tells us _____.

A. a young man's love story

B. a story that happened on a Father's Day

C. a heart-to-heart talk between a father and his daughter

D. a man in the true sense is one who is willing to face his own fear and responsible for all of his actions

5. The tone of the passage is _____.

   A. ironic   B. sad   C. humorous   D. serious

II. Decide whether each of the following statements is true or false. Put "T" for true and "F" for false in the space provided.

_____1. The author felt confused when the caller said she was Jenny.

_____2. Having answered all questions, the author was no longer puzzled or confused.

_____3. It is implied in the passage that he often dated girls when he was a teenager.

_____4. The author felt relieved the instant he knew the girl he dated was pregnant.

_____5. The author's real purpose of flying home to start searching is to take responsibility for all of his actions done at young age.

Passage 4

Traditions of Easter

Since its conception as a holy celebration in the second century,   1

Easter has had its non-religious side. In fact, Easter was originally a pagan festival.

The ancient Saxons celebrated the return of spring with an uproarious festival commemorating their goddess of offspring, Easter. When the second-century Christian missionaries (传教士) encountered the tribes of the north with their pagan celebrations, they attempted to convert them to Christianity. They did so, however, in a clandestine manner. The missionaries cleverly decided to spread their religious message slowly throughout the populations by allowing them to continue to celebrate pagan feasts, but to do so in a Christian manner.

2

As it happened, the pagan festival of Easter occurred at the same time of year as the Christian observance of the Resurrection (复苏) of Christ. So the modern spelling Easter appeared.

3

The Date of Easter Prior to 325 AD, Easter was variously celebrated on different days of the week, including Friday, Saturday, and Sunday. In that year, the emperor Constantine issued the Easter Rule which stated that Easter would be celebrated on the first Sunday that occurred after the first full moon on or after the vernal equinox (春分). However, the "full moon" in the rule is the ecclesiastical (教会的) full moon, which is defined as the fourteenth day of a tabular lunation (阴历月), where day 1 corresponds to the ecclesiastical New Moon. The ecclesiastical "vernal equinox" is always on March 21. Therefore, Easter must be celebrated on a Sunday between the dates of March 22 and April 25.

4

The Lenten Season Lent is the 46-day period just prior to Easter Sunday. Before that, there is a celebration, sometimes

5

called "Carnival (狂欢节)", practised around the world. It was designed as a way to "get it all out" before the sacrifices of Lent began.

The Cross   In 325 AD, Constantine decreed that the Cross was the official symbol of Christianity. The Cross is not only a symbol of Easter, but more widely used, especially by the Catholic Church, as a year round symbol of their faith.

6

The Easter Bunny   The Easter Bunny (小兔子) is the symbol originated with the pagan festival of Easter. The goddess, Easter, was worshipped by the Anglo-Saxons through her earthly symbol, the rabbit. Later the Germans brought the symbol of the Easter rabbit to America.

7

The Easter Egg   The Easter Egg predates the Christian holiday of Easter. The exchange of eggs in the springtime is a custom that was centuries old when Easter was first celebrated by Christians. Eggs were often wrapped in gold leaf or, if you were a peasant, colored brightly by boiling them with the leaves or petals (花瓣) of certain flowers.

8

Today, children hunt colored eggs and place them in Easter baskets along with the modern version of real Easter eggs—those made of plastic or chocolate candy.

9

(479 words)

How fast do you read?
　479 words ÷ _____ minutes = _____ wpm

Exercises for Passage 4

I. Decide whether each of the following statements is true or false. Put "T" for true and "F" for false in the space provided.

_____1. Easter was originally a religious festival.

_____2. It was missionaries who converted the ancient Saxons to Christianity.

_____3. The date of Easter was finally decided on a certain day.

_____4. The Cross, the Easter Bunny and Easter Egg are three symbols of Easter which were originated from ancient time.

_____5. It was Germans who brought the symbol of the Easter rabbit to America.

II. Complete each of the following sentences with the most appropriate word chosen from the box. Change the form if necessary.

commemorate	coincide with	convert to	correspond to
decree	observance	prior to	uproarious

1. This memorial _____ those who died in the war.
2. The governor _____ a day of mourning.
3. I called on her _____ my departure.
4. His tastes and habits amazingly _____ those of his wife.
5. The coach insists on the _____ of training rules.
6. His expenses don't _____ his income.
7. They burst into _____ laughter.
8. He solemnly _____ communism.

Unit 2

Olympics

> The most important thing in the Olympic Games is not winning but taking part; the essential thing in life is not conquering but fighting well.
>
> —*Pierre de Coubertin*

Passage 1

Ancient Olympics

The Olympic Games, originally created to honor Zeus, were the   1
most important national festival of the ancient Greeks, and a focus
of political rivalries between the nation-states. However, all

competitions involved individual competitors rather than teams. Winning an Olympic contest was regarded more highly than winning a battle and was proof of personal excellence. The winners were presented with garlands, crowned with olive wreaths. They were viewed as national heroes and on returning to their cities their countrymen pulled down part of the walls for them to enter. They were also given special privileges and high office.

Although records of the Olympics dated back to 776 BC when the Olympics were reorganized and the official "First Olympiad" was held, Homer (荷马), an ancient Greek blind poet, whose masterpiece *Iliad* (《伊利亚特》) suggested that they existed as early as in the 12th century BC. The games were held every four years in honor of Zeus, in accordance with the four year time periods which the Greeks called Olympiads. Emperor Theodosius I (狄奥多西一世) of Rome discontinued them in 393 AD, and they did not occur again until they were revived in Athens in 1896.

2

Originally, the Olympics were confined to running, but by the 15th Olympiad, additional sports were added: the pentathlon (five different events), boxing, wrestling, chariot racing, as well as a variety of foot races of varying lengths, including a long-distance race of about 2.5 miles.

3

Athletes usually competed nude, proudly displaying their perfect bodies. Women, foreigners, slaves, and dishonored persons were forbidden to compete; women, once they were married, were not even allowed to watch any Olympic events, except for chariot races. However, every four years, women held their own games, called the Heraea after Hera (宙斯之妻), held at Argos (古希腊国), and beginning as early as the 6th century BC, and lasting at least six centuries until Roman rule.

4

Unlike our modern Olympic Games, the ancient Greek Olympic   5
Games were a religious rather than secular festival, celebrating
the gods in general and Zeus in particular. The contests
themselves alternated with altar rituals and sacrifices, as well as
processions and banquets. Individual competitors were trained
rigorously not only for personal glory, but also to impress and
please a god through demonstrating strength and agility (敏捷).

Although one legend suggests that Heracles won a race at   6
Olympia and decreed that races should be instituted every four
years, the most common legends suggest that Zeus originated
the games after he defeated Cronus (宙斯之父) in battle.

(408 words)

How fast do you read?
408 words ÷ _____ minutes = _____ wpm

Exercises for Passage 1

I. **Choose the best answer for each of the following items in accordance with the passage.**

1. Besides enjoying great honor, the winners of the ancient Olympics

   _____.

   A. would be granted certain special advantages
   B. would be appointed to high position
   C. both A and B
   D. could violate the nation's law without being published

2. When were several additional sports added to the ancient Olympics?

    A. Until 836 BC.   B. Until 716 BC.

    C. Until 333 AD.   D. Until 453 AD.

3. Compared with the modern Olympic Games, the ancient Olympics were uniquely characterized by the following features EXCEPT _____.

    A. individual competitors rather than teams were involved in the ancient Olympics

    B. garland instead of metal medals were awarded to the winners in the ancient Olympics

    C. the ancient Olympics were more of a religious festival than a worldly one

    D. the ancient Olympics were held every four years

4. In the fifth paragraph, the author tries to tell us that _____.

    A. the ancient Olympics carried with deep religious spirit, which is quite different from the modern Olympics

    B. the ancient Olympic Games were held to celebrate the Olympian gods, especially in honor of Zeus

    C. God worship was part of the modern Olympics

    D. the individual competitors of the ancient Olympics were supposed to win the Games to impress and please the gods

5. It can be inferred from the last paragraph that the origin of the ancient Olympics was _____.

    A. definite   B. indefinite

    C. unknown   D. off the record

II. Decide whether each of the following statements is true or false. Put "T" for true and "F" for false in the space provided.

_____1. There were strict restrictions about who had right to participate in the ancient Olympics.

_____2. Opinions about when the ancient Olympics originated were controversial.

_____3. The ancient athletes usually competed naked in order to show their fit and good-shaped bodies.

_____4. The ancient Greek women were not entitled to take part in any games.

_____5. During the ancient Olympics, the religious activities and contests were held by turns.

Mascots Promise a "Friendly" Olympics

Beijing has unveiled its five 2008 Olympic mascots (吉祥物) —the "Five Friendliness" to coincide with the 1,000-day countdown to the big event. It is the first time in Olympic history that five mascots have been chosen. Each mascot has a rhyming two-syllable name, the traditional way of expressing affection for children in China. Beibei is the Fish, Jingjing is the Panda, Huanhuan is the Olympic Flame, Yingying is the Tibetan Antelope and Nini is the Swallow. The first characters of their two-syllable names read "Beijing Huanying Ni," or, in English, "Welcome to Beijing."

1

"The mascots are a special gift that Beijing presents to the world and to the Olympic Movement," said Liu Qi, president of the Beijing Organizing Committee for the Games of the XXIX Olympiad (BOCOG). The mascots, together with the official emblem and slogan of the 2008 Games, express Chinese people's wishes for peace, friendship, progress and harmony, Liu

2

said. The mascots have distinctive Chinese characteristics, representing not only the multi-ethnic cultures of China, but also the traditional Chinese philosophy of harmony between humans and nature, Liu noted.

Chosen in line with the colors of the Olympic Rings, they embody the landscape, dreams and aspirations of people from every part of China. They also represent the five elements of nature—the sea, forests, fire, earth and sky all stylistically rendered in ways that reflect the deep traditional influences of Chinese folk art and ornamentation (装饰).

3

"Five" also matches the five elements (metal, wood, water, fire and earth) believed by ancient Chinese people to explain the origins of the world. The "Five Friendlies" combine human and animal images. It is the first time that an Olympic element, the Olympic flame, has been included in the mascots.

4

Competition was hot with 662 entries, of which 611 were from the Chinese mainland, 12 from Hong Kong, Macao and Taiwan, and 39 from abroad. Many places wanted their local symbols picked as mascots.

5

China's western Qinghai Province pushed hard for the endangered Tibetan antelope, Fujian Province touted the South China tiger, Gansu favoured the mythical dragon and Jiangsu promoted the legendary Monkey King.

6

The "Five Friendlies" and other Olympic mascot merchandise will be on sale in authorized outlets in Beijing and other major Chinese cities.

7

The first mascot appearing at an Olympics was during the 1968   8
Winter Games in Grenoble, France, although Schuss the skier
was not official. The first official mascot was Waldi, the
Dachshund, who appeared at the Munich Summer Games in
1972. Since then, the mascots have become a main element of
the Olympic image. They have acted as a vehicle to convey the
Olympic spirit to the general public, especially to children.

(442words)

How fast do you read?

442 words ÷ _____ minutes = _____wpm

Exercises for Passage 2

**I. Decide whether each of the following statements is true or false.
Put "T" for true and "F" for false in the space provided.**

_____1. Every one of the five mascots embodies a lovely kind of animal.

_____2. According to the first paragraph, we can infer that the five 2008
Olympic mascots were made known to the world on 12th,
November, 2006.

_____3. So far, the 2008 Olympic mascots are the largest in number in
Olympic history.

_____4. The "Five Friendliness" are designed in a manner of combination
of man and animal images so as to represent a harmonious
relationship between man and nature.

_____5. China takes much care in choosing 2008 Olympic mascots in that
the mascots express not only Chinese people's good wish for
world development, but also some oriental characteristic culture
of China.

II. Translate the following sentences from the passage into Chinese.

1. They also represent the five elements of nature—the sea, forests, fire, earth and sky—all stylistically rendered in ways that reflect the deep traditional influences of Chinese folk art and ornamentation.

   _____

   _____

2. They have acted as a vehicle to convey the Olympic spirit to the general public, especially to children.

   _____

   _____

3. The mascots have distinctive Chinese characteristics, representing not only the multi-ethnic cultures of China, but also the traditional Chinese philosophy of harmony between humans and nature, Liu noted.

   _____

   _____

*P*assage 3

Amsterdam Olympics 1928

In 1928, the first modern Olympic Games came to Amsterdam   1
and all the women who competed there were under pressure to
preserve their modesty. Clothing was an issue for them all. The
British gymnastics team of 1928 were heavily criticized when they
posed for their team photograph revealing too much of their
shapely legs. On no account were they to show their knees, even

in thick black stockings! They were required to dress modestly, and wore black stockings under gym tunics when they made their competitive Olympic debut (初次登场) in Amsterdam. Even the team photograph showing crossed legs was frowned upon! It was not decent to show any contours (轮廓) or any womanly shapes (a difficult problem as many of the 1928 gymnasts were married women and not, as today, prepubescent (青春期前的) girls) and so the women had to bind their breasts with wide bandages while competing. Blouses underneath their tunic and ties helped the British women to conceal their bodies even more. This probably didn't help their movement and may explain why the gymnasts at this time were not performing somersaults (翻筋斗). The first Gold medal for team gymnastics in 1928 was won by the Netherlands, with Italy taking silver and Great Britain bronze. Ethel Seymour of Great Britain became the oldest gymnastic medalist winning her bronze at the age of 46 years and 6 months. A distinction unlikely to be seen today!

Despite the old concerns about women preserving their modesty and not showing too much of their bodies they all found creative solutions! One German athlete Leni Junker said: "We had to bring with us our own shoes and stockings and a shovel to dig foot holes for the start. We secretly cut our shorts which we thought were too long." "My uniform was white top and black bloomers to the knee and long black stockings. I cut the bottom of my bloomers on the ship over to Amsterdam." One of the Dutch 800-meter athletes once said, "We wore orange woollen shorts that we knitted ourselves.... Old gents said how outrageous it was—a woman in shorts!"

2

At that time women took part in the games in their restrictive athletics clothing. Although their clothing was made long enough

3

to cover them, they were fully aware of the shock they were causing by their dress—but it is worth bearing in mind that women running in shorts is still unacceptable in many cultures today. Also other different things were still left in these women's mind. "I'm a bit ashamed to tell you that my greatest memory from Amsterdam was that the men from the Mexican team followed the blue eyed girls from Sweden everywhere, and threw roses over them!" One of Sweden's women athletes said.

(456 words)

How fast do you read?
   456 words ÷ _____ minutes = _____ wpm

Exercises for Passage 3

I. Choose the best answer for each of the following items in accordance with the passage.

1. In 1928 Amsterdam Olympics, women gymnasts were criticized mainly for _____.
   A. their old age
   B. their poor performance
   C. their poor clothing
   D. revealing too much of their womanly shape
2. According to the passage, in 1928 Amsterdam Olympics, the women athletes participating in the competition were required to _____.
   A. bind their breasts with wide bandages
   B. report their names first
   C. dress modestly, and wore black stocking under gym tunics

D. dress formally

3. What does the phrase "frowned upon" (Line 10, Para.1) mean?

    A. Bring the eyebrow together.   B. Disapprove of something.

    C. Agree on.   D. Laugh at.

4. How do you understand the sentence "women gymnasts found creative solutions"?

    A. They brought all staff needed in the games and changed their clothing by themselves.

    B. They took part in the games by paying for fares by themselves.

    C. They ignored what others thought about them.

    D. They created their own skills in performing gymnastics.

5. Which of the following is NOT true according to the passage?

    A. Women gymnasts were required to dress modestly.

    B. Because of tight blouses underneath their tunic and ties, the women gymnasts were not allowed to perform somersaults.

    C. At that time, a woman in shorts was unacceptable.

    D. Women athletes weren't fully aware of the shock caused by their dress.

II. Translate the following sentences from the passage into Chinese.

1. On no account were they to show their knees, even in thick black stockings!

2. Even the team photograph showing crossed legs was frowned upon!

3. At that time women took part in the games in their restrictive athletics clothing.

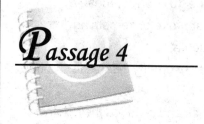

Olympic Torch and Flame

The torch is a symbol of the harmony and goodwill which represents the ideals of the Olympic Games. The Olympic flame represents the basic spiritual significance of the Olympic Movement, a symbol of peace among peoples of the world.

1

The torch is usually carried hand-to-hand by relays of runners from the original site of the Olympic Games at Olympia, Greece, to the main stadium of the current Games. This tradition started with the Berlin Olympic Games in 1936. To carry the torch during any part of its journey is considered a great honor. In Los Angeles, for the Games of the XXIII Olympiad in 1984, the torch relay route covered 15,000 kilometers. The route took 82 days and 3,636 runners participated. Interested persons were able to run for one kilometer by paying $3,000. In this manner more than $10 million were raised to benefit youth sports organizations.

2

The lighting of the Olympic flame at the site of the games is an important part of the opening ceremonies. Bringing the torch into the Games stadium is both a culminating as well as a beginning event. The Olympic flame ends its journey by lighting the Olympic torch of the Games. At the end of the games the flame is extinguished, but this signifies the beginning of the next

3

quadrennial (每四年一次的) and preparations for the next Olympic Games. In the modern era, the Olympic flame was lit for the first time at the 1928 Olympic Games in Amsterdam.

Torch ceremony, with its ritual and symbolism sets the Olympic Games apart from other sports events; it adds aesthetic (美学的) beauty to the competition of the Games. Baron Pierre de Coubertin, the father of the Modern Olympics, concluded that the torch ceremony had four specific traits: 1) historical meaning; 2) an educational message; 3) artistic appeal; 4) religious essence.

4

Historically, the most common use of the torches was to shed light in darkness, especially for travelers at night. Instructively, or educationally, the message for mankind was to teach people fair-play and instill a high regard for cooperation and togetherness. Artistically, the torch enhanced the elegance of the ceremonies. Finally, the religious essence derives from the first Olympic Games in 776 BC when young boys raced 200 yards to win the privilege of lighting the sacrificial altar fire honoring the Greek God Zeus (宙斯).

5

Throughout the succeeding years, the torch ceremony has changed, but its symbolism has not. The flame is borne throughout the world using many kinds of transportation until it reaches its destination.

6

(431 words)

How fast do you read?

   431 words ÷ _____ minutes = _____ wpm

Exercises for Passage 4

I. Decide whether each of the following statements is true or false. Put "T" for true and "F" for false in the space provided.

_____1. The ideals of the Olympic Games are harmony and goodwill.

_____2. The torch is carried hand to hand by relays of runners from every country of the world.

_____3. The lighting of the Olympic flame at the site of the games is the most important part of the opening ceremonies.

_____4. The torch ceremony is of great significance in history, education, art and religion.

_____5. At the end of the games, the extinguishment of flame signified the beginning of the next quadrennial and the preparations for the next Olympic Games.

II. Complete each of the following sentences with the most appropriate word chosen from the box. Change the form if necessary.

culminate	elegance	essence	extinguish
Participate	privilege	symbol	trait

1. The lion is _____ of courage.

2. His behavior _____ the last traces of affection she had for him.

3. The two arguments are in _____ the same.

4. We admired the _____ of the lady's clothes.

5. The Christmas party at school _____ in the distribution of the presents.

6. I always reserve to myself the _____ of changing my mind.

7. The old man actively _____ in the mass sports activities.

8. Anne's generosity is one of her most pleasing _____.

Unit 3

Exploration

> The process of scientific discovery is, in effect, a continual flight from wonder.
>
> —*Albert Einstein*

Passage 1

Cigarette Causes Blindness

Cigarette packets should carry warnings that smoking causes blindness, doctors will argue this week as a new study shows that the habit can badly damage eyesight.

A European study is set to show the leading cause of blindness—

1

2

age-related macular (有斑点的) degeneration-is directly attributable to smoking in more than one in four cases. In addition, clouding of the eye lens occurs in smokers 10 to 15 years earlier than in non-smokers.

"There are many thousands of smokers who have no idea that smoking can actually rob you of your sight," said Nick Astbury, president of the Royal College of Ophthalmologists. "The chemicals affect blood vessels throughout the body, and one of the secondary effects is that they slowly damage the tissues of the eye." 3

For years, cigarette packets have carried health warnings linking cigarettes to heart disease, cancer and harm to unborn babies. Now eye specialists will call for cigarette packets to carry warnings about blindness. A report, so far unpublished, on 5,000 patients across the European Eye Study shows that 27 percent of them had eye disease directly attributable to smoking. Other studies show that passive smoking can lead to eye diseases. 4

Simon Kelly, consultant ophthalmic (眼科的) surgeon, who has campaigned for awareness of the risks, carried out research last year in which he asked 400 patients about the links between illness and smoking. Although 90 percent realized the habit could cause lung cancer, fewer than 10 percent knew smoking could cause blindness. 5

"The evidence is so strong now that smoking really does harm the eye," said Kelly. "In the case of macular degeneration, we know smokers have a twofold to threefold risk of developing the condition. But if they also have a genetic predisposition to the disease, which becomes an eightfold increased risk." He called 6 for a campaign aimed at younger people. "In Australia and New Zealand, they ran a TV campaign spelling out that blindness could be caused by cigarettes, and that led to 72 percent of the population accepting that there was a link."

With macular degeneration, damage occurs because chemicals in tobacco affect the metabolism (新陈代谢) of the retina (视网膜) and bring about a premature aging of the eye. People risk gradually losing their central vision and could go completely blind.   7

There are two forms of the disease, "dry" and "wet" macular degeneration. In Britain, 250,000 people suffer from the wet type, which is linked to smoking and is partly caused by leakage of fluid. Some people don't lose their sight entirely, but find they can no longer read or drive. It mostly affects people over 60, but in some cases where there are genetic factors it can occur in middle age.   8

(453 words)

How fast do you read?
    453 words ÷ _____ minutes = _____wpm

Exercises for Passage 1

I. Choose the best answer for each of the following items in accordance with the passage.

1. According to a European study, which of the following is true?
    A. One fourth of blindness cases is caused by smoking.
    B. Smoking can cause blindness.

C. The leading cause of blindness is related to age.

D. More than 25 percent of blindness cases are directly caused by smoking.

2. According to Nick Astbury's explanation, the cause of blindness is

_____.

A. the chemicals in tobaccos affect blood vessels throughout the body and slowly damage the tissue of the eye

B. the chemicals in tobacco can actually rob human of sight

C. the chemicals in tobacco affect the metabolism of retina

D. the chemicals in tobacco bring about a premature aging of eye

3. Why did eye specialists call for cigarette packet should carry warnings about blindness?

A. Because smokers ask them to do so.

B. Because more and more people had eye disease directly attributed to smoking and passive smoking can lead to eye disease.

C. Because eye specialists want to warn teenagers not to smoke.

D. Because more and more people fall in the habit of smoking.

4. The phrase "campaigned for "(Line 2, Para. 5) is closest in meaning to

" _____ ".

A. took part in

B. called for

C. led a movement for

D. looked for

5. According to the passage, which of the following is NOT true?

A. Smoking habit can badly damage eyesight.

B. Eye specialists have realized the harm of smoking to human's eyesight.

C. More and more people have realized the harm of smoking to human's eyesight.

D. The passage mainly tells that smoking is harmful to human's eyesight.

II. Translate the following sentences from the passage into Chinese.

1. A European study is set to show the leading cause of blindness—age-related macular (有斑点的) degeneration—is directly attributable to smoking in more than one in four cases.

   _____

   _____

2. The chemicals affect blood vessels throughout the body, and one of the secondary effects is that they slowly damage the tissues of the eye.

   _____

   _____

3. With macular degeneration, damage occurs because chemicals in tobacco affect the metabolism (新陈代谢) of the retina (视网膜) and bring about a premature aging of the eye.

   _____

   _____

Passage 2

Our Nuclear Lifeline

Mother Earth is in trouble. Every time we click a light switch or start a car, something sinister happens. From power station chimneys and car tail-pipes, immense volumes of gases such as carbon dioxide (CO_2) are pumped into the sky where they pollute

1

the environment and act like a greenhouse, over-heating the globe. The ever-rising temperature will cause dramatic physical changes, such as rising sea levels, flooding of coastal cities and landscapes.

But there's a lot we can still do to forestall disaster. Global warming stems from our dependence on carbon-based fuels such as coal, oil and natural gas. If only we could avoid burning these "fossil" fuels, global warming would lose momentum. But how could we possibly do that?   2

A lifeline does exist, and it is dangling in front of us. By grasping it now we can reduce the world from both the consequences of global warming and our looming energy shortages. It's safe, proven, practical and cheap.   3

Our lifeline is nuclear energy. Nuclear feeds on about two truck-loads of cheap and plentiful uranium (铀) imported from stable countries like Canada or Australia. Gas and acid emissions: zero. Toxic ash and dust: none. High-level radioactive waste produced: a few bucketfuls.   4

The benefits of using nuclear energy instead of fossil fuels are overwhelming. We know nuclear energy is safe, clean and effective because right now, 438 nuclear reactors are supplying almost one-seventh of the world's electricity.   5

Most fears about nuclear power center on radiation. Yet it's part of our natural environment and we can live with it. All of us are exposed to natural radioactivity every minute, mostly from rocks and soil. The radiation bombarding us goes up 10 percent when we sleep next to another human. A weekend at a beach with   6 granite rocks could increase it more than two-fold and possibly by even more in a week's skiing holiday.

How do nuclear power stations compare? According to the UK's National Radiological Protection Board, doses from the entire nuclear industry amount to less than one percent of our total exposure. Medical uses such as X-rays account for 14 percent and the remainder is natural. Compared with known cancer risks such as smoking and poor diet, it reports, the risk from non-medical, man-made radiation is about 1/100th of one percent.

7

The figures show that many people's instinctive fears of nuclear energy are unreasonable. The few accidents to occur are vastly exaggerated.

8

(403 words)

How fast do you read?
   403 words ÷ _____ *minutes =* _____ *wpm*

Exercises for Passage 2

I. Choose the best answer for each of the following items in accordance with the passage.

1. Which of the following is NOT cited as an instance of causing global warming?
   A. Using air-conditioner in summer.
   B. Generating electricity from power plant.

C. Getting a car started.

D. Turning on a light.

2. The author's opinion about nuclear energy in slowing down the pace of global warming and relieving energy shortages could be best described as _____.

A. sympathetic   B. pessimistic

C. optimistic   D. critical

3. Why is nuclear energy considered as lifeline in the view of the author?

A. Because source of burning fuel is available at a low cost.

B. Because it does little harm to environment either with regard to poisonous gas emission or produced waste.

C. Because it's safe and effective concerning the low risk of radiation.

D. All the above.

4. By "live with it" (Line 2, Para. 6), the author suggests that _____.

A. man ought to accept the fact and endure it since radiation is inseparable from human's living environment

B. man can't adjust themselves to living under radioactive environment

C. man can't live under radioactive environment

D. radioactivity does no harm to human

5. Several comparisons have been made in the last second paragraphs of the passage to prove that people's fear of the occurrence of nuclear radiation accidents is _____.

A. necessary   B. overstated   C. understated   D. sensitive

II. **Decide whether each of the following statements is true or false. Put "T" for true and "F" for false in the space provided.**

_____1. The day for coastal cities to be flooded is coming soon if we do nothing about global warming.

_____2. Global warming and energy crisis are getting serious on a daily basis.

_____3. Once we use nuclear energy instead of burning fossil fuels, global warming will come to a stop.

_____4. It's fear of radiation that frightens people not to use nuclear
energy.

_____5. Contrary to common people's belief, much of radiation comes
from natural radioactivity.

Passage 3

Dogs Smell Cancer in Patients' Breath

Dogs can detect whether someone has cancer just by sniffing the
person's breath, a new study shows.

1

Ordinary household dog with only a few weeks of basic "puppy
training" learned to accurately distinguish between breath
samples of lung-cancer and breast-cancer patients and healthy
subjects.

2

The study provides convincing evidence that cancers hidden
beneath the skin can be detected simply by dogs examining the
odors of a person's breath. Early detection of cancers greatly
improves a patient's survival chances, and researchers hope that
man's best friend, the dog, can become an important tool in early
screening.

3

Lung cancer and breast cancer patients are known to exhale(呼出)
patterns of biochemical markers in their breath. Cancer cells emit

4

more different metabolic waste products than normal cells. The differences between these metabolic products are so great that they can be detected by a dog's keen sense of smell, even in the early stages of the disease.

The researchers used a food reward-based method to train five ordinary household dogs. Encountering breath samples captured in tubes, the dogs gave a positive identification of a cancer patient by sitting or lying down in front of a test station.   5

By scent alone, the dogs identified 55 lung and 31 breast cancer patients from other 83 healthy humans. The results of the study showed that the dogs could detect breast cancer and lung cancer between 88 and 97 percent of the time. The high degree of accuracy remained even after results were adjusted to take into account whether the lung cancer patients were currently smokers. "It did not seem to matter which dog it was or which stage cancer it was, in terms of our results," Broffman said.   6

According to James Walker, director of the Sensory Research Institute at Florida State University in Tallahassee, canines' (犬类) sense of smell is generally 10,000 to 100,000 times superior to that of humans.   7

It is unclear what exactly makes dogs such good smellers, though much more of the dog brain is devoted to smell than it is in humans. Canines also have a greater convergence of neurons (神经元) from the nose to the brain than humans do.   8

"The dog's brain and nose hardware is currently the most sophisticated odor detection device on the planet," McCulloch, the study leader, said. "Technology now has to rise to meet that challenge."   9

"Researchers envision (预想) that dogs could be used in doctors'　　10
offices for preliminary treatments," Walker said. "This could be an
experimental diagnostic tool for a while, and one that is
impossible to hurt anyone with or to mess up their diagnosis with."

Broffman hopes to build on the current study to explore the　　11
development of an "electronic nose." "Such technology would
attempt to achieve the precision of the dog's nose," he said. "Such
technology would also be more likely to appear in your doctor's
office."

(476 words)

How fast do you read?
　　476 words ÷ _____ minutes = _____ wpm

Exercises for Passage 3

**I. Choose the best answer for each of the following items in accordance
with the passage.**

1. In Para. 2, the author uses the word "subjects" to refer to "_____."
　　A. people undergoing the experiment
　　B. patients
　　C. courses of study
　　D. samples
2. Why can dogs detect cancer just by sniffing the patient's breath as the
　　study shows?
　　A. Because dogs boast of a fairly keen sense of smell.

B. Because cancer cells give off different metabolic waste products that can be sensed by dogs.

C. Because dogs have already received certain period of special training.

D. All the above.

3. Which of the following was NOT mentioned as a result of the study?

A. The study showed that dogs are great helpers in detecting cancers.

B. The rate of accuracy remained high even taking smoking into consideration.

C. Dog species or stage of the patient's cancer took little effect on the valid of the experiment.

D. It's easier for dogs to detect lung cancer than breast cancer.

4. It is implied in the last paragraph that _____.

A. the dog's brain and nose are the most developed organs in the world

B. at present, man has already invented one odor detection device superior to dog's brain and nose

C. under the present circumstances, technology lags behind dog's brain and nose in terms of odor detection

D. in no time, scientists will develop one kind of odor detection device more sophisticated than dog's brain and nose

5. The passage is mainly about _____.

A. a new study result that dogs can smell cancer just by sniffing the patient's breath

B. the methods of how to train dogs to detect cancer

C. the reasons why dogs are good at smelling

D. the relation between dogs and high technology

II. Translate the following sentences from the passage into Chinese.

1. Ordinary household dog with only a few weeks of basic "puppy training" learned to accurately distinguish between breath samples of lung- and breast-cancer patients and healthy subjects.

   _____

   _____

2. The high degree of accuracy remained even after results were adjusted to take into account whether the lung cancer patients were currently smokers.

   _____

   _____

3. It is unclear what exactly makes dogs such good smellers, though much more of the dog brain is devoted to smell than it is in humans.

   _____

   _____

Passage 4

Bug Detectives

Forensics (法医学) has always used anything that science can give us to cope with various crimes. But forensics has always had its limits. In fact there are major factors in any murder that 21st century science still cannot crack. Crucially, for example, even

1

with all our technology, it is impossible for forensic science to estimate the time of death when a body is found more than 72 hours after a murder. For a body that has lain for more than a few days, guesswork is the best forensics that can do in telling us how long ago a person was murdered. But, over 100 years ago, two disciplines came together entomology (昆虫学), the study of insects, and forensics, the scientific analysis of crime. But it is only now that this remarkable discipline, Forensic Entomology, is coming into its own and solving the unsolvable.

Dr. Dorothy Gennard is a Senior Lecturer in Biological Science at Lincoln University. To study what happens to a human body after death or murder, scientists like Dr. Gennard experiment on pigs. The carcass (尸体) of any animal is of intense interest to insects. The first on the scene, within minutes of death, is the common housefly. She quickly decides if the carcass will be a good place to lay her eggs, so that when they hatch, they will have a convenient source of food. When the fly lays its eggs, it starts a biological clock ticking. The lifecycle of egg to maggot(蛆) to adult fly takes place over a known period of time usually 10 days. By identifying what stage the insect is at, experts can estimate its age and relate this to how long the body has been dead.   2

Dr. Dorothy Gennard said, "If a body has been found and it is covered in maggots then we can go back and we can identify what species of maggot that is. And we can work out how old that maggot is and therefore the period of time since colonization (移生) of the body."   3

Creatures like flies give us that opportunity to determine that post-mortem (死后的) interval at a period later than the pathologist(病理学家) can. The pathologist can tell us how long the person has   4 died up to about 72 hours quite accurately, from there the entomologist is able to add a further dimension. By timing the biological clock of insect activity backwards, virtual clues can be discovered about the time of death.

Britain's most distinguished forensic entomologist, who has helped solve over 500 criminal cases during 27 years, is Dr. Zakaria Erzinciolglu. And in case after case, he is pinpointing (准确描述) time of death months and even years after the death took place, solving murders or mysteries.   5

(459 words)

How fast do you read?

   459 words ÷ _____ minutes = _____ wpm

Exercises for Passage 4

I. Decide whether each of the following statements is true or false. Put "T" for true and "F" for false in the space provided.

_____1. Forensics has succeeded in solving crimes of any type.

_____2. Over a hundred years ago, Forensic Entomology has already been applied to solve the unsolvable crimes.

_____3. The biological clock of the eggs of the insect plays an important role for scientists to estimate how long the body has been dead.

_____4. Forensic Entomology is more effective than traditional detective methods in solving crimes that happened over 72 hours ago.

_____5. The passage is mainly about how scientists have made well use of insects to detect crimes.

II. Translate the following sentences from the passage into Chinese.

1. Forensics (法医学) has always used anything that science can give us to cope with various crimes. But forensics has always had its limits.

   _____

   _____

2. The carcass (尸体) of any animal is of intense interest to insects.　The first on the scene, within minutes of death, is the common housefly. She quickly decides if the carcass will be a good place to lay her eggs, so that when they hatch, they will have a convenient source of food.

   _____

   _____

3. By timing the biological clock of insect activity backwards, virtual clues can be discovered about the time of death.

   _____

   _____

Unit 4

Education

The roots of education are bitter, but the fruit is sweet.

—*Aristotle*

Passage 1

Top of the Class

Finnish schools were not only at the top academically among OECD (the Organization for Economic Cooperation and Development) countries, but also succeeded better in educating less gifted pupils and significantly reducing academic difference between boys and girls. To put it simply, Finnish schools left no child behind.

1

So just what did the Finns do right? The answer is certainly not lavish spending. Finland's expenditure on primary and secondary education is slightly higher than the European average but lower than some of its Nordic neighbors. Nor has Finland relied on nostrums touted by educators in other countries, such as aggressive testing, heavier workloads, an emphasis on back-to-basic, or tougher discipline. Finns, virtually all of whom attend public schools, actually begin their schooling later than students elsewhere—at seven—and spend an average of just 30 hours per week on schoolwork, including homework. This compares to 50 hours per week spent by Korean students, whose achievements level was just behind Finland's on the PISA test assessment.

2

Problems that harass schools in many countries are relatively rare in Finland. Although bullying, drug use and disrespect for teachers exist, they are dealt with as early as possible and absenteeism is also rare. Of some 62,000 secondary-school graduates each year, only about 1,000 drop out and half of them eventually return to complete their course.

3

Indeed Finland does have some modest advantages. It has few immigrants with problems of language and cultural adjustment. Finland also enjoys a long tradition of national literacy. During centuries of Swedish and Russian rule, reading and writing Finnish became a symbol of nationalism and a matter of pride.

4

Until the mid-1970s, however, Finland was hardly a model of scholastic innovation. As in many European countries, Finnish students were separated by examination at the age of ten onto parallel academic or vocational tracks. This shaped the rest of their lives, since it was almost impossible to switch from one track to the other once the assignment had been made.

5

Critics argued that if Finland were to compete successfully in a
changing economy world, the education system would have to be
overhauled. "In the new knowledge-based society it is much
easier for highly educated population to be retrained for new
professions," says Leo Pahkin, a senior advisor for the National
Board of Education. To ensure that the entire population has
access (途径) to education and training is the main aim of the
Finnish education system. The principle of lifelong learning, the
idea that people are always capable of learning new things at all
stages of life, is an important principle for all education provision
(规定), from basic schooling to adult education.

6

(442 words)

How fast do you read?

442 words ÷ _____ minutes = _____ wpm

.

Exercises for Passage 1

**I. Choose the best answer for each of the following items in accordance
with the passage.**

1. Finnish schools have accomplished great achievements EXCEPT
   _____.

   A. Finnish students occupy a high position among OECD countries in
   terms of aptitude for study
   B. Finnish schools have done a good job in educating less talented pupils
   C. Finnish schools have been successful in narrowing gender difference
   in education
   D. Finnish schools managed to ensure that no child has dropped out

2. Which of the following factors attributes to Finnish schools' success in education?

    A. Finnish government's heavy investment in education.

    B. Finnish school's dependence upon some popular teaching value promoted by educators.

    C. No harassing problems existing in Finnish schools.

    D. Practice of education reform in an era of "knowledge economy".

3. With what topic is the passage mainly concerned?

    A. Why are Finnish schools at the top of the class?

    B. Is it necessary to reform education in a knowledge-based society?

    C. How do Finnish schools educate students?

    D. How do Finnish schools come to be a model of scholastic innovation?

4. The word "overhauled" (Line 3, Para. 6) most probably means "_____".

    A. overtaken

    B. examined carefully and made necessary adjustment

    C. overthrown

    D. overturned

5. According to the passage, which of the following statement is NOT true?

    A. Bias is unreasonable and unacceptable in Finnish educators' conception of teaching.

    B. Large amount of time devoted to study is not an absolute and necessary factor for a child's academic success.

    C. It's not until the mid-1970s that the Finnish educators began to reconsider their education system.

    D. Students should be regrouped by examination at an early age to decide whether to receive academic or vocational education.

II. Translate the following sentences from the passage into Chinese.

1. The answer is certainly not lavish spending. Finland's expenditure on

primary and secondary education is slightly higher than the European average but lower than some of its Nordic neighbors.

_____

_____

2. Although bullying, drug use and disrespect for teachers exist, they are dealt with as early as possible and absenteeism is also rare.

_____

_____

3. During centuries of Swedish and Russian rule, reading and writing Finnish became a symbol of nationalism and a matter of pride.

_____

_____

Passage 2

Internet Plagiarism

Giving or receiving any inappropriate assistance on an exam is cheating, whether it involves sneaking a look at your neighbor's test or scribbling notes on your palm. In recent years, however, some of these old-fashioned techniques have given way to a new trend: Internet plagiarism. ("Plagiarism is a form of stealing. At school it usually involves taking someone else's ideas of work and claiming that is your own.")

1

Every day, thousands of students copy phrases, paragraphs, and whole pages from the Internet, then try to pass those words off as

2

their own work. This cut-and-paste practice has been made easy by the availability of term papers and source documents on the Web.

Since the Internet becomes readily accessible to students in the 1990s, it has become in some ways the educator's worst enemy. In secondary schools and universities alike, students are taking advantage of the fact that ready-made papers are only a few clicks away. An entire industry has sprung up to provide free homework—or at a price—papers purported (声称) to be custom-made.

3

Now teachers are fighting back. Across the country, educators have become savvier about using a combination of in-class writing samples, Internet search engine, and anti-plagiarism technology to beat the cheating scourge.

4

For schools that choose the low-tech way to fight plagiarism, taking in-class writing samples is one of the easiest solutions. Teachers simply ask students to write a few paragraphs, which they hand in immediately.

5

But many schools are turning to technological solutions like Turnitin. The online tool, created by iParadigms of Oakland, CA, in 1988, searches the Internet as well as millions of publications for copied passages as short as eight words. It scans papers against material that has collected from professors to check papers against one another, and see if any two students have plagiarized from the same site.

6

At schools that haven't invested in technology like Turnitin, teachers are developing their own strategies for detecting plagiarism. In three and a half years of teaching English at Brooklyn College, Damian Da Costa caught two to three students each year by

7

searching for phrases from their papers with Google.com.

Elisabeth Tully, the director of a school library, focuses more on   8
plagiarism prevention than punishment, pointing out that schools
must be vigilant about ensuring that students understand what
plagiarism is and how they can avoid it.

"It is not even so much that they're cutting and pasting electronic   9
stuff," she says. "They may have had written something out of a
book, but if they didn't at the same time assign a source code and
put the right quotations around it, they might make a mistake and
inadvertently plagiarize."

(447 words)

How fast do you read?
   447 words ÷ _____ minutes = _____ wpm

Exercises for Passage 2

I. **Choose the best answer for each of the following items in accordance
   with the passage.**

1. By "pass those words off as their own work" (Lines 2-3, Para.2), the
   authors means that _____.
   A. students intend to rewrite those words
   B. students assume those words as their own work
   C. students try to find out the password for those words
   D. students try to take off those words from their own work
2. What has made Internet plagiarism easy according to the passage?

A. The appearance of personal computer.

B. Accession to term papers and source documents on the Web site

C. Free charge of term papers and source documents on the Web site.

D. The widespread of on-line education.

3. Facing Internet plagiarism trend, educators have become _____ in fighting back.

A. more helpless   B. more confident

C. more concerned   D. wiser

4. Based on Director Elisabeth's comment, which of the following is NOT true?

A. In fact, educators needn't make a fuss about students' "cutting and pasting" practice.

B. Informing students of what plagiarism is and ways to avoid it are more effective than "catch-and-punish" in preventing Internet plagiarism.

C. Being lack of knowledge of what plagiarism is, students might unintentionally fall in the trap of plagiarism.

D. It's advisable that school should do more in plagiarism prevention than punishment.

5. The passage is mainly about _____.

A. introduction of Internet plagiarism

B. introduction of ways of fighting against Internet plagiarism

C. how teachers fight against Internet plagiarism

D. what ways teachers should adopt in fighting against Internet plagiarism

II. Decide whether each of the following statements is true or false. Put "T" for true and "F" for false in the space provided.

_____1. Traditional cheating techniques in exam such as peeking at neighbor's test or scribbling notes on palm are not seen any longer since the appearance of Internet.

_____2. Educators have come to terms with the new trend of Internet plagiarism.

_____3. Educators have adopted integrated methods in beating the cut-and-paste practice instead of single one.

_____4. All schools don't turn to Turnitin for help in fighting against Internet plagiarism.

_____5. Research has proved high-tech like Turntin is more effective than low- tech means in fighting against Internet plagiarism.

Passage 3

Boys' Struggle with Reading and Writing

While girls may have overcome the gender gap in science and math at school, recent research from around the world shows boys continue to struggle with reading and writing. "We always knew that girls were doing quite well in the areas of literacy and languages and writing," said Reynolds, a researcher. "But there was not a great deal of concern about boys because boys were always getting the better jobs and salaries."

1

Boys used to have an advantage over girls in math and science. But recent science and math testing has shown any performance gap that once existed between boys and girls in those subjects has all but disappeared in Canada. Some even speculate that next year, the girls may move ahead of the boys in the council test in science, which puts the girls squarely in the lead when it comes

2

to university entrance or achievement in the labor market.

In a culture that favors equal opportunity and advocates political correctness, some have found it's difficult to discuss this troubling gender gap without entering into the touchy (难以处理的) domain of sexism. Reynolds, an educator cautioned it is important to address differences between boys and girls without assigning blame.

3

Some say boys continue to lag behind in writing and reading because of the "feminization" of education. Increasingly, teaching is becoming dominated by women, which leaves boys with few male role models in the classroom.

4

Factors of girls' proclivity (倾向) to be more verbal and boys' desire to be more active may also contribute to the problem. Other experts said the kinds of reading materials available in schools may better suit girls than boys. Boys' reading preferences include concrete facts and instructional material that will help them better understand a particular area of interest, whereas girls are more attracted to stories that explore interpersonal relationships.

5

In Canada, there are a variety of approaches to level out skill levels at school. For example, students are being encouraged to read material of their choice together in small mixed-gender groups, followed by a discussion project that allows participants' choices including illustrator, group leader or summarizer.

6

But some argue the only way to ensure equitable treatment of boys and girls in the education system is to segregate them. There are also key differences in the way boys and girls respond to confrontation. Girls shrink away from a confrontational teaching style under which many boys would thrive.

7

Educator Reynolds argues the study of brain function is a   8
relatively new science which is barely understood and shouldn't
form the basis for education policy. "I don't think we have to get
overly concerned," she said. "I think we do have to pay attention
to what we're doing in our homes with our boys and in our
classrooms with our boys and that there may be things we could
do differently, and better, and these scores could actually change."

(479 words)

How fast do you read?
   479 words ÷ _____ minutes = _____ wpm

Exercises for Passage 3

**I. Choose the best answer for each of the following items in accordance
with the passage.**

1. It was generally believed that girls were doing quite well in the fields of

   _____.

   A. communicating and writing
   B. math and science
   C. reading and writing
   D. writing and science
2. From the 2nd paragraph, we can conclude _____.
   A. boys are spoiled by their parents
   B. boys weren't always ignored
   C. boys are good at getting better jobs and better salary than girls
   D. boys had an advantage over girls in getting better jobs and better
      salaries in the past
   3. According to the passage, as the performance gap in math and

science between boys and girls disappeared, some predict that

_____.

  A. girls will become superior to boys as far as university entrance or achievement in the labor market are concerned

  B. girls will not worry about employment

  C. more girls will enter colleges and universities

  D. more girls will not get married

4. Which of the following is NOT true according to the passage?

  A. There will be more and more female teachers.

  B. Boys like female teachers.

  C. Girls are more attracted to stories that explore interpersonal relationship.

  D. Some experts said the kinds of reading materials available in school may better suit girls than boys.

5. The passage mainly tells _____.

  A. there is no way to change the fact that boys continue to lag behind in writing and reading

  B. the fact that boys continue to lag behind in writing and reading exists, but efforts must be made to change the trend and to diminish the gender gap in education

  C. gender gap exists between boys and girls

  D. boys are good at science and math, whereas girls are good at literacy and language

II. Translate the following sentences from the passage into Chinese.

1. Some even speculate that next year, the girls may move ahead of the boys in the council test in science, which puts the girls squarely in the lead when it comes to university entrance or achievement in the labor market.

_____

_____

2. Some say boys continue to lag behind in writing and reading because

of the "feminization" of education.

_____

_____

3. But some argue the only way to ensure equitable treatment of boys and girls in the education system is to segregate them.

_____

_____

Passage 4

When Your Child Hates School

If a child seems depressed or anxious about school, fakes illness to stay home, repeatedly winds up in the nurse's or principal's office, or refuses to talk about large chunks of the school day, you should be concerned. 　　1

Here are some of the most common reasons that kids hate school and strategies to put them back on the road to success: 　　2

Anxiety　One fear that keeps children from enjoying school is separation anxiety. It most frequently occurs when a child is about to enter a new school. Parents should learn how to lessen the anxiety by the way they respond. A firm "Have a great day, and I'll pick you up at 2:30!" is more confidence-inspiring. You can help 　　3 your child handle fearful situations—from speaking up in class to taking tests—by rehearsing (排练) at home.

Loneliness Some kids dislike school because they have no friends. This may be the case if your child is always alone, feigns illness to avoid class outings or gives away treasured possessions in an attempt to be liked. Often loneliness problems can be solved by bolstering social skills. You might teach a young child a few "friendship openers," such as "My name's Tom. What's yours? Do you want to play tag?" Teachers should let kids who are very lonely tell anything good about themselves.

4

Bullies If your child seems quiet and anxious, has few school friends or suddenly shows a drop in self-esteem, he may be a victim of a bully. The common advice for this problem—teach your child to be assertive (自信的)—isn't always enough. In elementary school children should tell a teacher. In middle school and above, kids should stick with friends and avoid places where the bully hangs out. If you have to step in, go to the principal, not the bully's parents.

5

Trouble Learning Some children's school complaints spring from physical problems. For example, vision problems. Parents need to be sensitive to signs of trouble. Get your child a complete vision exam. Kids with learning disabilities often get frustrated, fail to finish assignments or appear to ignore the teacher. If you suspect your child has a learning disability, you can ask the teachers about having an evaluation by the school psychologist.

6

Poor Chemistry with a Teacher What if your child constantly complains that a teacher is "unfair" or "mean"? Sometimes the solution is simple. "Having the teacher and child sit down for lunch together can often improve the relationship," observes Carole

7

Kennedy, former president of the National Association of Elementary School Principals.

Remember, kids know how to play a parent against a teacher. So if your child tells you a horror story about school, don't automatically assume you're getting the whole truth. Talk with the teacher, principal or guidance counselor. Once you identify why your child hates school, you can almost always find a solution.   8

(478 words)

How fast do you read?

478 words ÷ _____ minutes = _____ wpm

Exercises for Passage 4

I. Choose the best answer for each of the following items in accordance with the passage.

1. To lessen separation anxiety, _____.
    A. parents should speak more encouraging words when parting with their kid
    B. parents should help children handle fearful situations by practice at home
    C. parents should help their kids to get self-confident
    D. all the above
2. According to the passage, in order to overcome loneliness, _____.
    A. children must learn some social skills
    B. parents should help children bolster social skills and teachers should encourage lonely children to tell anything good about themselves
    C. children ought to avoid class outings

　　D. children ought to give away treasured possessions in an attempt to be liked

3. According to the passage, when child becomes a victim of a bully, _____.

　　A. parents should keep silent

　　B. parents can transfer their child to another school

　　C. parents can teach the bully a good lesson

　　D. none of the above

4. From Para. 6, we know that _____.

　　A. some children's complaints result from physical problems

　　B. vision problems are the main factors leading to learning trouble

　　C. psychologist can handle children's physical problems

　　D. parents need to be sensitive to children's learning problems

5. "Poor Chemistry with a Teacher" (Line 1, Para. 7) is closest in meaning to "_____".

　　A. good relationship with a teacher

　　B. close relationship with a teacher

　　C. poor relationship with a teacher

　　D. obscure relationship with a teacher

II. Decide whether each of the following statements is true or false. Put "T" for true and "F" for false in the space provided.

_____1. The passage mainly tells us some common reasons why some kids hate school as well as strategies to tackle these problems.

_____2. When kids dislike school, they feel lonely.

_____3. According to the passage, physical problems may result in learning trouble.

_____4. Teacher's unfairness is also one of the reasons leading to children's dislike of school.

_____5. The last paragraph suggests parents should believe everything that kids tell them.

Unit 5

Man and Animal

> They are the creatures that are always there to remind us we are not alone. And somehow, their animal presence makes us more human.
>
> —*Author Unknown*

Passage 1

Circus Animal

For many, the word "circus" evokes imagery of popcorn, candy, "wild" animals, and fun. But this fun is at a high price when there are animals involved. Ever wonder how circuses manage to get the animals to perform so well? In fact, Animals do not perform

1

the acts you see in the circus naturally. They have to be trained, often by extreme methods. They are injured into obeying their human trainers' commands. Bull hooks are often driven into the tender areas of an elephant's body to make it cooperate. Electric shock, whips, baseball bats and pipes are also among the methods used to force the animals to cooperate in training. Some animals are kept muzzled (戴上口罩) to force them and discourage them from defending themselves if they feel threatened. Some animals are drugged to make them manageable and some have their teeth removed. Some bears have had their paws burned to force them to stand on their hind legs.

Besides, the living condition of circus animal is unfavorable, too. Most animals used in the circus are meant to live in the wild. Instead of their natural habitats where they would roam free and live on their natural instincts, they are forced to live and travel in cramped quarters far smaller than their habitats in the wild. They are often forced to eat, sleep and even defecate in the same place. Circuses travel to many locations and water is limited in some locations, bathing and cleaning the animals' living quarters is given low priority where water is limited. Unfortunately, this limitation extends to their drinking water as well. Many circuses give no consideration to climate and the animals are exposed to extreme heat or cold. In addition, their diets do not consist of what they would naturally eat and they are sometimes underfed in the interest of getting an ideal performance. Disease is common among circus animals. Veterinarians (兽医) qualified to treat exotic animals are not always present and circus animals frequently suffer inadequate veterinary care. 2

The combination of the above circumstances and other factors lead to mental distress in circus animals. There have been many 3 cases of animals' attacking humans and escaping. When you think about how they are treated, can you blame them for attacking? What might they think of humans? They don't ask for the miserable lifestyle circus performance subjects them to.

Training doesn't necessarily have to create problems for their wellbeing (身心健康), provided that the circus animals are taught by means of reward and provided that animals are used that don't mind performing, like dogs. The display of tricks is a routine occupation for animals and this can only be seen as acceptable when an animal trainer respects the fact that animals sometimes don't want to perform. It would be a good thing if humans spontaneously (自发地) paid due respect to animals. Respect should lead to a more harmonious world.

4

(483 words)

How fast do you read?
483 words ÷ _____ *minutes =* _____ *wpm*

Exercises for Passage 1

I. Choose the best answer for each of the following items in accordance with the passage.

1. This passage mainly talks about _____.
   A. the sufferings of circus animals
   B. the worsening living condition of circus animals
   C. the fact that circus animals are suffering from serious mental distress

D. how circuses manage to get the animals to perform well

2. Which of the following is true with regard to circus animals?

A. Circus animals' performances are too funny.

B. Circus animals are born to perform those thrilling acts as we see in the circuses.

C. Under the force of extreme methods and brutal tools, not only do circus animals suffer from physical problems, but also from mental distress.

D. Much attention has been paid to the circus animals' living condition.

3. What's the author's attitude towards how circus animals have been trained?

A. Critical.   B. Neutral.

C. Enthusiastic.   D. Ironic.

4. The word "underfed" (Line 13, Para. 2) probably means "＿＿＿＿＿".

A. no food to eat   B. a little food to eat

C. enough food to eat   D. not a little bit food to eat

5. It can be inferred from the passage EXCEPT ＿＿＿＿＿.

A. the author calls on that circus should be banned on behalf of wild animals

B. it's against natural law to train wild animals to perform acts people want to watch

C. disease often spread among circus animals for lacking of skillful native veterinarians

D. circus animals' mistreatments justify the cases of their attacking humans or escaping

II. Translate the following sentences from the passage into Chinese.

1. Circuses are supposed to be for fun, children love them. But this fun is at a high price when there are animals involved.

＿＿＿＿＿＿＿＿＿＿＿＿＿＿＿＿＿＿＿＿＿＿＿＿＿＿＿＿＿＿＿＿＿＿＿＿＿

＿＿＿＿＿＿＿＿＿＿＿＿＿＿＿＿＿＿＿＿＿＿＿＿＿＿＿＿＿＿＿＿＿＿＿＿＿

2. Instead of their natural habitats where they would roam free and live on their natural instincts, they are forced to live and travel in cramped quarters far smaller than their habitats in the wild.

_____

_____

3. Many circuses give no consideration to climate and the animals are exposed to extreme heat or cold.

_____

_____

Passage 2

A Hero and an Angel

Rick and Vicki Tarter had recently lost their beloved boxer (拳师犬) to cancer when they applied to our non-profit organization, Boxer Rescue, asking to adopt a boxer dog.   1

The Tarters passed all our stringent requirements to adopt Odie: a boxer that apparently closely resembled their deceased pet. Odie was a very handsome boxer and even better than that, he was a very nice boxer. He got along well with every person and every dog he met, although he really preferred not to keep company with cats! We were thrilled when the Tarters came along and were very happy when they chose Odie and took him home.   2

As our contract states, Vicki took Odie to her veterinarian (兽医) to   3 have him evaluated soon after they got him home. To our surprise, Odie was positive for heartworms. Odie was given the painful and risky injection to kill the heartworms and then he was kept very still and quiet at home with the Tarters.

After a month, he was taken back to his vet to be checked and was free of the heartworms. Life was just beginning again for Odie, and Rick and Vicki had fallen head over heels in love with this sweet boy. We were thrilled that he was living "the good life." But as often happens, it didn't last long.　　4

On July 5, 2005, the Tarters were away from home. Their teenage son was sleeping and somehow a fire broke out in the house. Odie quickly woke the boy up and alerted him to the fire. When the son tried to get Odie to come out of the house, Odie would not follow. Instead, he went to Rick and Vicki's room, presumably to be sure they were not in the house. The fire was too hot and the son was unable to get Odie out.　　5

Odie died in that fire that day. The house was a total loss, but when Vicki called me the following day, it was Odie she was crying for. She told me how she had grown to love him; how sweet and loving he was. Vicki was obviously still in shock over her losses.　　6

It is so ironic to me that Odie was saved from death by a needle and he saved the life of one of the humans who loved him. I don't know what Odie's life was like before he found himself in the shelter, but I know he was very loved and well cared for in the short time he lived with the Tarters. I truly believe Odie became a hero the same day he became an angel.　　7

(434 words)

How fast do you read?

434 words ÷ _____ minutes = _____ wpm

Exercises for Passage 2

I. Choose the best answer for each of the following items in accordance with the passage.

1. Why did the Tarters choose to adopt Odie as their new pet?
   A. Because they were required to adopt him.
   B. Probably because Odie was such a handsome and nice boxer.
   C. Probably because they fell in love with Odie at the first sight.
   D. Probably because Odie looked very much like their formal boxer, together with his cute appearance and nice temper.
2. Why was Odie not willing to go out of the house after he had warned the son of the big fire?
   A. Because the fire was too big to go out at that time.
   B. Because Odie thought the Tarters might have been in their room.
   C. Because Odie knew the Tarters were at home.
   D. Because it's a habit of Odie to go out together with the Tarters.
3. The phrase "head over heels" (Line 3, Para. 4) is closest in meaning to
   "_____".

   A. wrongly   B. down-to-earth
   C. seriously   D. deeply
4. It can be inferred from the passage that _____.
   A. Odie was a deserted boxer
   B. even the employee of the Boxer Rescue was greatly moved by Odie's heroic deed
   C. it is safe for Odie to take an injection to be cured of the heartworms
   D. it is ironic for the writer that Odie lived a short life after having been

injected

5. The story was narrated in _____.
 A. the first person   B. the second person
 C. the third person   D. unknown

II. Decide whether each of the following statements is true or false. Put "T" for true and "F" for false in the space provided.

_____1. The Tarters' former boxer died of cancer.

_____2. A series of strict requirements had to be passed before adopting any animal from the Boxer Rescue organization.

_____3. Odie was a boxer rescued by the Boxer Rescue organization from a shelter.

_____4. It seemed that Odie was willing to be together with cats.

_____5. The author added a quotation on the phrase "the good life" in that Odie actually did not live a happy life in the Tarters' family.

Passage 3

A True Treasure

My horse, Treasure, is my hero because she helped me discover how to relate to her. In the process, she "fixed" my relationship with my husband and my children.

I have had horses all my life. I was very good at manipulating them, with ropes, bits, bats and spurs, and making them do what I wanted. Everyone knows you have to show the horse who is boss.

Well, I was also a lot like this in my personal life, very demanding, very authoritarian, very one-sided.   3

When I got this mare, she was a fiery (暴躁的) 2-year-old, with no   4
handling. She was not going to accept any type of dictatorship from me. In the interest of not getting myself killed, I started to read and educate myself on ways to manage a high-spirited horse. I had a lifetime of experience: I had been raising and breaking horses since I was a teen, and I had never encountered another creature who would not bend to my will.

I discovered natural horsemanship, a method of training that   5
focuses on communication. In order to communicate with another person, you must be understood. The very definition of understanding is two or more individuals sharing the same idea. This simple definition had a big impact on me. I realized (suddenly, after twenty years) that communication is a two-way street!

When I started applying natural horsemanship concepts to my life,   6
I noticed a change in the way other people related to me. My husband, when I stopped ordering him around, became happier and more helpful. My children, when I practised being fair, firm and most of all, consistent, were motivated to respond sooner, at the polite request from me rather than the orders I used to issue.

I think the most valuable life skill I learned from my horse is that   7
pressure motivates, but release teaches. As soon as I incorporated these basic skills into my daily activities, I started to

notice positive changes. My children were more considerate of each other, and stared to ask first, without telling. I became acutely aware of my position as a role model.

My extreme mare was not hard to catch, she would stand grooming and saddling without being tied and she was much safer to have around my children. This positive effect snowballed on a daily basis. Today, five years later, I have the perfect horse. I also have very polite, considerate kids and a very happy husband. There is nothing in the world that can compare to being adored by the ones you love most—even if it all started with the attitude of a very special horse.

8

(439 words)

How fast do you read?
439 words ÷ _____ minutes = _____ wpm

Exercises for Passage 3

I. Answer the following questions with the information you get from the passage.

1. How did the author use to tame horses?

_____

_____

2. Why did the author start to read and educate herself on ways to manage a high-spirited horse?

_____

_____

3. What is "natural horsemanship" defined as by the author?

_____

_____

4. What payoff has the author got when applying natural horsemanship concepts to her personal life?

_____

_____

5. How to paraphrase the sentence "This positive effect snowballed on a daily basis."?

_____

_____

II. Decide whether each of the following statements is true or false. Put "T" for true and "F" for false in the space provided.

_____1. Treasure is regarded as a hero by the author for the simple reason that it helps her discover how to establish a good relationship.

_____2. Treasure is too ill-tempered to get along with.

_____3. The author's former relationship with her families was not as good as present.

_____4. It can be inferred from the passage that the author used to order issues to her families as to what to do and how to do.

_____5. Nowadays, communication is of much importance to the author and her families, together with her horse.

Passage 4

The Cars in Dog Heaven
Have No Wheels

Buford was not as dumb as his name might imply. Well, sometimes he wasn't, anyway. For a while, he ran with a bad crowd—the dogs from down the road that took to killing the sheep across the river. We knew that our dog was just scavenging (清除) what the others had killed; we also knew the sheep's owner would have every reason and right to rid himself of any canine (犬的) scourge (灾祸), even ours.

1

So we started chaining Buford up when we weren't home. It was a long chain, but still cooped up all day in the driveway with only three trees to play with. Buford would sometimes scramble up, to stand and drool amid the few large, lopped-off branches before skittering down to wave his long feathery tail at us as we cheered.

2

One bright fall day as my step-dad was splitting firewood on the porch, Buford came to watch. Chop went the ax. Wag went the tail. Then a chop and a wag and a FLOP. Half the tail laid on the porch. The dog didn't make a sound, only looked up beseechingly (恳求地), trying to figure out how he'd deserved this terrible blow.

3

Then there was the kitten. Those days, we always had around a

4

dozen barn cats in various stages of frailty and disrepair. Evidently Buford thought so, too. They were always curled up together or playing somewhere. Their favorite game was catching. Buford often carried the kitten around in his mouth—the little thing lying luxuriously across the dog's bottom jaw; then he'd stop and flip it gently into the air and catch it again. The kitten, dizzy as it got, seemed to love it. Then Buford would set it down, amazingly gently for such a big dog. Once back on land, the kitten would dance drunkenly for a moment before pressing up against Buford's leg in affection.

One day, a game of catch went wrong. The kitten's neck was broken; it died in an instant. Buford laid it softly underneath the tree where we'd been playing. He howled and cried, in that awful primeval way that made the hairs on your arms stand up. We buried the kitten under the tree, where Buford sat for weeks, every day, rain or shine.   5

Eventually he recovered, and put new energy into another favorite game: chasing our truck. The house sat far back from the highway, on the trailing edge of a blind corner. The driveway was long enough to have its own streetlight. In the winter, the snow would fall and Buford would jump and twist and bite at the snowflakes' shadows.   6

After a couple of years at our rented farmlet, we moved back to town. Buford stayed with an uncle in the country, where his car-Chasing habit finally did him in. But there is a dog heaven, isn't there? For certain kittens, too.   7

(478 words)

How fast do you read?

478 words ÷ _____ minutes = _____ wpm

Exercises for Passage 4

I. Decide whether each of the following statements is true or false. Put "T" for true and "F" for false in the space provided.

_____1. We chained Buford when we weren't at home in case that the sheep's owner should kill him.

_____2. Buford always chased the kitten until it stopped running.

_____3. Buford and the cat enjoy playing together.

_____4. Buford was so sad for the kitten's death that he sat under the tree for weeks without eating anything.

_____5. Buford died of car-chasing.

II. Answer the following questions with the information you get from the passage.

1. What would Buford often do when we chained him up?

_____

_____

2. Can you describe the deep feelings between Buford and the kitten?

_____

_____

3. What does the title mean?

_____

_____

Unit 6

Growing Up

> The problem is not that there are problems. The problem is expecting otherwise and thinking that having problems is a problem.
>
> —*Theodore Rubin*

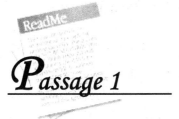

Passage 1

Don't Be Afraid of Worry

Monsters under the bed. A thunderstorm. The dark. All young   1
children worry about things, real or imagined. And as they grow,
so do their anxieties. Will the kids on the soccer team like me?
Will I pass tomorrow's test? Most parents manage to console their

kids and lessen their fears. But for some children, anxiety crossed the line from normal to unhealthy.

One child can't eat for fear of choking. Another has a fear of animals. Or she dreads going to school because she hates being away from Mum all day. Children often suffer on their own because they don't recognize that they have a problem, don't understand what's happening to them or can't explain their feelings. Parents might overlook or minimize their children's problems. Or they might have trouble interpreting the signs—children can express anxiety in many ways, from extreme shyness to irritability or even defiance (公然反抗). Fortunately, here, too, parents can develop strategies to help anxious children cope.

2

Worries are a part of growing up and being grown-up. It's normal and even healthy for children to worry a little: It gives them the tools they need to withstand life's bumps and spills. "The butterflies in the stomach before a school play or a big test would motivate a child to work hard and do her best," says Marie Cumming, a marriage and family therapist.

3

If a worry meter existed, healthy anxiety presents challenges that children learn from, and it makes them resilient (性格开朗). A little higher on the meter, however, would be worries that distress children rather than challenge them. A child with such anxiety has fears she can't conquer; for example, the knots in her stomach prevent her from being able to get out of the car just before a big soccer game. Kids with this type of anxiety need more help: perhaps some professional intervention such as family therapy (治疗). At the top of the anxiety meter would be the extreme but relatively uncommon anxiety disorders that prevent children from

4

successful day-to-day living, such as the child who is so afraid of dirt that she washes her hands several times an hour. These kids require more intense professional therapy and, quite often, medication.

Here are some ways to overcome worry:　　　　　　　　　　5

- Face your fears;
- Talk openly about your unique feelings and fears and nip anxiety in the bud as soon as possible;
- Don't feel overwhelmed by too many activities;
- Enforce proper sleep and dietary;
- And lastly, encourage yourself to take risks and face increasingly complex challenges so that you will feel good of yourself.

(445 words)

How fast do you read?
　445 words ÷ _____ minutes = _____ wpm

Exercises for Passage 1

I. Choose the best answer for each of the following items in accordance with the passage.

1. Sometimes children themselves would become worry-makers if they _____.

　A. fail to notice that they are having a problem

77

      B. fail to comprehend what's happening to them

      C. fail to make their feelings understood

      D. all the above

2. What's the author trying to tell us in Para. 3?

      A. If controlled properly, the unavoidable worries are beneficial to kids' growing up.

      B. It is common for kids to worry a lot during growing up.

      C. Worries are of great use for kids to grow up and to be grown up.

      D. Kids should get worried before a school play or a big test.

3. Both idioms "butterflies in the stomach" (Lines 3-4, Para. 3) and "knots in one's stomach" (Line 5, Para. 4) means _____.

      A. calmness   B. nervousness

      C. sensitivity   D. sadness

4. Healthy worry is beneficial to kids' growing up EXCEPT _____.

      A. it equips them with necessary tools to resist life's failures or become discouraged

      B. it motivates them to work hard and do them best

      C. it presents challenges that they can learn from, and makes them easily and quickly get recovered from hardship or suffering

      D. it helps them get full ready to conquer the whole world

5. According to the passage, besides parents' participation, what's required to help excessively anxious children to overcome worry?

      A. Heart-to-heart talk.

      B. Professional therapy, including medication.

      C. Self-awareness.

      D. Take-it-easy attitude.

II. Decide whether each of the following statements is true or false. Put "T" for true and "F" for false in the space provided.

      _____1. Most parents have managed to comfort their kids or to relieve their worries.

_____2. At times, parents are partly responsible for their kids' unhealthy worries if they don't know how to handle them properly.

_____3. It is normal and even healthy for young children to worry about things, be they real or imagined.

_____4. Worries can never bring positive effects on children's growing up.

_____5. Parents are supposed to leave their worried kids alone as long as the children's anxiety is healthy.

Forgive

My mother was abusive(辱骂的), both physically and emotionally. She had very little patience and if I made a mistake or caused an accident she would strike me. In addition, she was constantly calling me stupid, an idiot, etc. I spent my entire childhood living in constant fear of doing something to displease her. As a result I seemed to be constantly doing things to displease her. I also lived with constant anger. My father, though patient and loving, was simply never available. Besides working very long hours, it seemed that when he was around, he was more interested in my brother than he was in me. I simply didn't seem to matter to him and was pretty much ignored.

1

I vowed that if I ever had children I would be the opposite of her. I did have children and struggled to do things differently. I found

2

that I also had little patience but kept reminding myself how destructive it would be to lash out at my children. Consequently my children, now adults, have memories of having had a lot of freedom to be themselves when they were growing up. I kept my vow to never physically hit my children or damage their egos by calling them names. When they were young I wouldn't allow my parents to spend much time with them for fear they would treat them as they had treated me.

For years I lived with all the anger, which depleted my energy and got in the way of my happiness. Gradually, I began to understand how my childhood affected my adulthood—but I was still not able to forgive my mother. I was in therapy for seven years and finally understood that it is not just a matter of understanding, it has more to do with resolution. During the therapeutic process, I was unconsciously resolving the anger little by little, though I didn't realize it. I talked to my mom about what I was learning in therapy. She very courageously listened and without any defensiveness, was able to apologize. She also shared things with me about her childhood and her marriage. Eventually, without even realizing it, I began to feel that my mother had a very difficult life and did not intentionally hurt me. She did the best she could under the circumstances. I no longer felt angry with her and was able to forgive her. We became very close and shared a very good relationship for the last 10 years of her life. When she passed away I was so grateful that I resolved the anger I once had and had the 10 years with her.

3

(441 words)

How fast do you read?

441 words ÷ _____ minutes = _____ wpm

Exercises for Passage 2

I. Decide whether each of the following statements is true or false. Put "T" for true and "F" for false in the space provided.

_____1. My mother had a little patience when I made a mistake or caused an accident.

_____2. Although my father was patient and loving, he was more interested in my brother.

_____3. I promised to be much more patient with children if I had my own ones.

_____4. For years I endured all the anger, which made my life happy.

_____5. At last I forgave my mother and kept a close relationship with her in her last 10 years.

II. Answer the following questions with the information you get from the passage.

1. Why didn't the author as a child feel to be loved either by her mother or her father?

_____

_____

2. How did the author treat her own children?

_____

_____

3. Why did the author forgive her mother at last?

_____

_____

Grandfather's Lunch

I was six years old. Aunt Trang, who was eight years older, was helping me get dressed. I was excited at the prospect of taking lunch to my grandfather. **1**

So hand in hand, with Aunt Trang carrying the lunch rack, we scurried one block down the road to our grandfather's place. **2**

It was 1974 and war was raging all over Vietnam, but in Tay Ninh(西宁) life continued as usual, though there were gunshots and mortar (迫击炮) explosions. **3**

Whhizzz! "Duck down!" Aunt Trang cried out as we walked along. Ratatatatat! Somewhere in the mountains just outside town, trigger-happy soldiers had decided it was a fine day to unleash their arsenal (兵工厂) of flying pellets down our path. "Stay low and take cover!" **4**

As we squatted at the side of the road, covering our heads, I started to worry about the food, which grandfather liked to be served hot. If we didn't get there on time and his lunch turned cold—oh, I dreaded the thought! I refused to let this outbreak of hostilities slow us down. "Let's just run for it!" I said. **5**

Aunt Trang suggested duck walking down the road. It wasn't a **6** good idea. After a few paces, my stubby (粗而短的) little legs began cramping.

We tried all the life-preserving maneuvers we could think of, running the gamut from practical to ridiculous. Nothing seemed to work, and we were ready to sit things out until the shooting was over. Then a lightning bolt of memory hit. If we ever came under fire, our elders had told us time and again, we should run from side to side. "Bullets travel in a straight line," they assured. "Run in a zigzag."   7

So taking a deep breath, we set off again, running wildly back and forth across the road. After what seemed an eternity of bullet dodging, the shooting stopped. "Buddha be praised, the food is still warm," was all I could say after we arrived at our grandfather's apartment, completely unaware of the danger we'd just survived. Five cents awaited each of us!   8

As an adult, I sometimes look back on that eventful day with a mixture of humor, immense gratitude and humility. I now know what my young mind couldn't grasp then: it's impossible to go through life without trials and struggles being thrown at you. They come when you least expect them; when your guard is down and your defenses are weak. They come when you're happily strolling down a street and bullets start flying at you.   9

You can dodge them all if you want, but as long as you're alive, they will keep coming, from all directions. You cannot always stop Death in your tracks, or duck down forever. Sure, you might get wounded, but you just have to bandage the wound and carry on. There's no room for complacency (自满) or defeat.   10

(499 words)

How fast do you read?
499 words ÷ _____ minutes = _____ wpm

Exercises for Passage 3

I. Choose the best answer for each of the following items in accordance with the passage.

1. In what tone did the author describe the soldiers' gun shooting on that day?
   A. Annoyed.   B. Humorous.
   C. Sad.   D. Frightened.
2. The word "dodge" (Line 1, Para. 10) probably means "_____".
   A. fight   B. run
   C. avoid   D. hit
3. What is "bullets" in the last two paragraphs metaphorically(暗喻) referred to?
   A. Difficulties, challenges and anything disagreeable.
   B. Gunshots.
   C. Flying pellets.
   D. Trials and struggles.
4. With what kind of feeling did the author as an adult recalled that eventful day?
   A. Fun.
   B. Great thankfulness.
   C. A combination of fun and great thankfulness.
   D. A combination of fun, appreciation and awareness of his failings.
5. It can be inferred from the passage that _____.
   A. war had no impact on ordinary people's lives at all during that

period

B. the author's grandfather was angry with him

C. the simple event of sending grandfather lunch deeply influenced the author's character-shaping and world outlook

D. life in Vietnam is dangerous, for when you are happily strolling down a street, bullets would start flying at you

II. Answer the following questions with the information given from the passage.

1. In what setting did the story take place?

_____

_____

2. Why did the author want to arrive at his grandfather's apartment on time?

_____

_____

3. What did the author and his aunt intend to do after a few unsuccessful trials?

_____

_____

4. How did the author finally manage to get his destination(目的地)?

_____

_____

5. What lesson does the author learn from the event of sending his grandfather's lunch?

_____

_____

Passage 4

Facing the Challenge

It was the worst thing that could happen to a spoiled ten-year old boy: eight o'clock in the evening, storm raging outside, much homework still undone, home all alone except for the maid working in the kitchen. I began to cry. Then the phone rang. I wiped my tears, swallowed my sobs and answered. It was my mother.

1

"Hello, Carlo?" she began. "I'm still…"

2

"Where are you?" I interrupted.

3

"I'm here, in Glori's, with your brother. Hail a tricycle and fetch us here," she said.

4

Stunned, I couldn't utter a word, although I knew the Glori's Supermart was only five minutes from our house. My mother continued.

5

"Carlo? Is that OK with you?"

6

"Sure, no problem," I replied.

7

"Great!"   8

I put the phone down. I couldn't believe I had said yes. I wanted to   9
call back to say I couldn't do it.

But then I stopped. Do grown men shrink away from challenges?   10
No, and I was a grown man. I resolved to face the challenge: To
commute to Glori's. Right then I felt like a cavalier (骑士) on a
quest, a knight in shinning armor sallying forth to succor (救援) a
lady and a child in distress. I put on my yellow raincoat and
stepped out of the house.

The chilly wind hit me in the face and the rain pounded me.   11
Lightning streaked across the sky and thunder boomed. I was
scared. I hadn't taken pubic transportation before. I started to walk
back to my house when tricycle pulled over beside me.

"Boy, do you need a ride?" the driver asked.   12

I hesitated. The driver wore a transparent raincoat ten sizes too   13
big and had a moustache. I remembered all those action films. I
wanted to say "No," but I knew I might not get another ride if I
turned this one away.

"Are you getting in or not?" the driver asked impatiently.   14

"Yes. To Glori's." I said finally.   15

As we pulled away, I became frantic with worry. Overwhelmed, I   16
began to pray. It didn't stop me from trembling, but it did ease my
fears. The minutes flew by. We reached Glori's.

My mother and my younger brother Paolo were standing just outside the main entrance. They saw me and walked towards me.   17

"Wow, you're really a big boy now, taking public transportation on your own," my mother said with a smile. We all got in. Paolo turned to me. "Carlo, you were really brave today," he said.   18

I smiled nonchalantly. "It was nothing. Someday you'll do this too." He looked at me as if I were a god.   19

I felt great. I had faced my fears. I had a brother who trusted me and a memory of a little adventure for keeping.   20

"Were you scared?" my mother asked me.   21

"Scared? Me?" I replied indignantly. "It was only a five-minute ride."   22

I looked at her. She was beaming.   23

(486 words)

How fast do you read?

486 words ÷ _____ minutes = _____ wpm

Exercises for Passage 4

I. Choose the best answer for each of the following items in accordance with the passage.

1. When the story happened, nobody was at home EXCEPT _____.
   A. the author himself
   B. the author and the maid
   C. the author's younger brother
   D. the author's mother and his younger brother

2. As time went by, the author began to cry. Why?
   A. Because he was hungry.
   B. Because he missed his mom.
   C. Because he felt scared.
   D. Because the lights went off.

3. Putting the telephone down, the author _____.
   A. immediately felt excited, and went out
   B. felt glad because his mother would come back soon
   C. wasn't scared any more because he knew where his mom was
   D. felt regretful for what he had said first, but soon he overcame his fear and resolved to face the challenge

4. Why did the author hesitate to take the tricycle when the driver asked him?
   A. Because he didn't like the driver.
   B. Because he thought the driver might be a bad guy.
   C. Because he was waiting for another tricycle to come.
   D. None of the above.

5. The author felt great in the end because _____.
   A. he had faced his fears and was admired by his younger brother
   B. he finally saw his mom

C. he had never felt scared

D. he thought he became brave

II. Translate the following sentences from the passage into Chinese.

1. I wiped my tears, swallowed my sobs and answered.

_____

_____

2. Right then I felt like a cavalier (骑士) on a quest, a knight in shinning armor sallying forth to succor (救援) a lady and a child in distress.

_____

_____

3. The chilly wind hit me in the face and the rain pounded me. Lightning streaked across the sky and thunder boomed.

_____

_____

4. I wanted to say "No," but I knew I might not get another ride if I turned this one away.

_____

_____

Unit 7

Health and Fitness

Passage 1

Unable to Fall Asleep Though Tired

Why is it so difficult to fall asleep when you are overtired? There is   1
not an answer that applies to each individual. But many people fail
to note the distinction between fatigue physical tiredness and
sleepiness, the ability to stay awake. It is possible to feel "tired"
physically and still be unable to fall asleep, because while your
body may be exhausted, you don't feel sleepy. To fall asleep, you

need adequate time to unwind, even if you feel fatigued. It is not so easy to simply "turn off".

According to Carl E. Hunt, director of the National Center on Sleep Disorders Research in Bethesda, Maryland, most people do not allow themselves sufficient deceleration.

2

Lack of sleep makes things even more complicated. Experts say adults need at least 7 to 8 hours of sleep a night to function properly. When you get less sleep than that on consecutive nights, you begin to accrue "sleep debt." As sleep debt increases and functionality decreases, your body experiences a stress response and begins to release adrenaline (肾上腺素). Now a vicious cycle has been created: you experience the feeling of being more and more tired, but your body is increasingly stimulated. "Power sleeping" for more hours on weekends is only a temporary solution. "There is no substitute for getting a good night's sleep on a regular basis," says Hunt.

3

Sleep is a natural and essential part of our existence. One sleep researcher calls sleep "the window of mental health", and the examination and treatment of sleep problems can be a first step in helping depressed and anxious people.

4

Here are some simple tips that many people have found helpful.

5

Do's...

6

- Make sure that your bed and bedroom are comfortable— not too hot, not too cold, not too noisy.
- Make sure that your mattress supports you properly. It should not be so firm that your hips and shoulders are

under pressure or so soft that your body sags. Generally, you should replace your mattress every 10 years to get the best support and comfort.

- Get some exercise. Don't overdo it, but try some regular swimming or walking. The best time to exercise is in the daytime — particularly late afternoon or early evening. Exercising later than this may disturb your sleep.
- Take some time to relax properly before going to bed. Some people find aromatherapy helpful.
- If something is troubling you, and there is nothing you can do about it right away, try writing it down before going to bed and then tell yourself to deal with it tomorrow.
- If you can't sleep, get up and do something you find relaxing. Read, watch television or listen to quiet music. After a while you should feel tired enough to go to bed again.

(464 words)

How fast do you read?

464 words ÷ _____ minutes = _____ wpm

Exercises for Passage 1

I. Choose the best answer for each of the following items in accordance with the passage.

1. The phrase "turn off" (Line 8, Para. 1) most probably means "_____".
   A. change direction
   B. turn off lights
   C. turn to sleeping from the state of being fatigued

D. remain awake

2. According to Para. 1, which of the following statements is true?

A. There is an absolute answer that applies to each individual's sleeping problem.

B. No difference exists between physical fatigue and sleepiness.

C. No more time is needed for over-tired people to fall asleep.

D. To fall asleep, over-tired people need enough time to relax themselves.

3. Adults would acquire "sleeping debt" if _____.

A. they sleep less than 7 to 8 hours now and then

B. they sleep less than 7 to 8 hours on successive nights

C. they sleep less than 7 to 8 hours only one night

D. they don't get a "power sleeping" for more hours on weekends

4. The author's attitude towards "power sleeping" is _____.

A. favorable   B. unfavorable

C. neutral   D. positive

5. It can be inferred from the 4th paragraph EXCEPT that _____.

A. depressed and anxious people have trouble in sleeping well with no exception

B. sleep is of vital importance to human being's wellbeing

C. poor sleep might be a hint of one's mental problem

D. enough sleep is one key in helping depressed and anxious people

II. Translate the following sentences from the passage into Chinese.

1. It is possible to feel "tired" physically and still be unable to fall asleep, because while your body may be exhausted, you don't feel sleepy.

_____

_____

2. Lack of sleep makes things even more complicated.

_____

_____

3. Now a vicious cycle has been created: you experience the feeling of being more and more tired, but your body is increasingly stimulated. "Power sleeping" for more hours on weekends is only a temporary solution.

_____

_____

Yoga

What comes into your mind when you hear the word Yoga?   1

Well, if you think of women in seemingly impossible poses, then   2
you may have an inkling of what Yoga is. You've got a long way to
go before fully understanding Yoga.

Yoga is an ancient Indian knowledge of body that dates back   3
more than 5,000 years ago. The word "Yoga" came from the
Sanskrit (梵文) word "yuj" which means "to unite or integrate."
Yoga then is about the union of a person's own consciousness
and the universal consciousness.

Ancient Yogis (瑜伽修行者) had a belief that in order for man to be   4
in harmony with himself and his environment, he has to integrate
the body, the mind, and the spirit. For these three to be integrated,

emotion, action, and intelligence must be in balance. This balance is mainly done through exercise, breathing, and meditation (静坐)— the three main Yoga structures.

Yoga has become so popular in recent years, it's easy to overlook the fact that it is actually one of humankind's oldest activities. Scholars think that yoga grew out of the methods used by shamans (巫师) of the Indus Valley, more than 5,000 years ago.

5

Shamans were the holy men of early human civilization. Their role in society was to communicate with the spirit world to find keys to problems facing their people. Over time, these shamans developed a system of mental and physical exercises to expand their consciousness, and thereby gave a new perspective on the problems of daily life. These exercises formed the base of modern yoga.

6

Yoga was practically unknown to the West until the 1960s, when popular culture began to show an interest in Eastern religions. People began to look at yoga as a way to find peace of mind in a world that was anything but peaceful.

7

Since the 1960s yoga's popularity has grown increasingly. Nowadays, Westerners practise different kinds of yoga. There is Bikram, or "hot yoga", done in rooms heated to over 40 degree Centigrade. There is baby yoga in which babies copy the stretching pose of their mothers. There are even yoga classes for people in their 70s.

8

Here are some reasons why more and more people are practicing Yoga:

9

- Yoga relaxes the body and the mind;
- Yoga can help normalize body weight;
- Yoga improves your resistance to disease;
- Yoga increases your energy level and productivity;
- Yoga leads to genuine inner ease of mind.

In fact, there are so many people who want to learn yoga that   10
yoga classes across the United States are having difficulty in
keeping up with the demand. Judging by its popularity, yoga is as
useful for solving the problems of today as it was for solving the
problems 5,000 years ago.

(457 words)

How fast do you read?
   457 words ÷ _____ minutes = _____ wpm

Exercises for Passage 2

I. **Choose the best answer for each of the following items in accordance with the passage.**

1. Which of the following is closest in meaning to the word "overlook" (Line 1, Para. 5)?
   A. Have a view from the above.   B. Pass over without punishment.
   C. Fail to see or notice.   D. Supervise (监督).
2. In the 1960s, Westerners began to look at yoga as a way to find peace of mind in a world that was _____.
   A. peaceful   B. prosperous
   C. quiet   D. hustle and bustle

3. Which of the following best summarizes the main idea of Para. 6?

   A. Shamans were the holy men of early human civilization.

   B. Shamans play an important role in ancient society.

   C. How was the base of modern yoga formed.

   D. How did shamans find keys to problems facing their people.

4. Which of the following kinds of yoga practised by Westerners is NOT mentioned in the passage?

   A. Hot yoga.   B. Senior citizen yoga.

   C. Baby yoga.   D. Teenager yoga.

5. It can be concluded from the last paragraph that _____.

   A. more and more Westerners show interest in yoga nowadays

   B. more and more Americans want to learn yoga that the supply of yoga school is out of demand

   C. yoga is useful for solving the problems of modern society as well as for the problems 5,000 years ago

   D. all the above

II. Answer the following questions with the information you get from the passage.

1. How has yoga gained its rapid popularity in recent years in modern society?

   _____

   _____

2. According to the professional views, when and where did modern yoga originate?

   _____

   _____

3. Did Shamans play an important role in the ancient Eastern religion?

   _____

   _____

4. Under what circumstances did yoga begin to be known by Westerners?

_____

_____

*P*assage 3

Compulsive Buying

Compulsive buying is just as common in men as in women, a nationwide telephone survey has found, and in its extreme forms, it may be a psychiatric (精神病学的) illness—an impulse (冲动) control disorder associated with abnormal levels of depression and anxiety.

1

Researchers used a seven-item questionnaire to determine whether people felt a need to spend money, whether they were aware that their spending behavior was abnormal, whether they bought things to improve their mood and whether their buying habits had led to financial problems.

2

They followed up with three questions designed to determine the degree of loss of control: How often have you just wanted to buy things and did not care what you bought? How often have you bought something and when you got home, but not sure why you bought it? How often have you gone on a buying spree and just

3

could not stop?

A statistical analysis of the results found that 5.5 percent of men
and 6.0 percent of women could be classified as compulsive
shoppers—that is, people whose uncontrolled urges to spend
money lead to serious negative consequences.

4

Compulsive buying, sometimes called compulsive or addictive
shopping, is not a recognized psychiatric diagnosis (诊断), but it is
now being considered for inclusion in the next edition of the
Diagnostic and Statistical Manual of Mental Disorders.

5

Dr. Lorrin Koran, the study's lead author said compulsive buyers
commonly suffer from other psychiatric disorders. "Many of those
who come in for treatment suffer from depression, anxiety
disorders and other impulse control disorders like pathological (病
态的) gambling and binge eating," Dr. Koran said.

6

An editorial published with the paper notes that the recognition of
such a condition as a mental illness would be controversial and
that some would criticize it as creating a trivial disorder in order to
"medicalize" a moral issue or to invent a reason to sell more
drugs.

7

"Compulsive buying, like pathological gambling, may lead to
bankruptcy, divorce, loss of employment and even suicide
attempts," Dr. Koran said.

8

The survey shows, surprisingly, that men and women are equally
or nearly equally likely to suffer from this disorder, and that a
troubling proportion of the population appears to be engaging in
financially destructive behavior. The authors acknowledge that

9

their results are based only on a telephone survey, which is subject to various biases, and that without a structured clinical interview, an accurate diagnosis is not possible.

Dr. Koran hoped that people who think they have this disorder will   10
seek help because available studies suggest that psychotherapy or medications help many compulsive buyers to stop.

(428 words)

How fast do you read?
   428 words ÷ _____ minutes = _____ wpm

Exercises for Passage 3

I. Choose the best answer for each of the following items in accordance with the passage.

1. How did the researchers carry out the research?
   A. By filling in forms on the spot.
   B. By filling in questionnaire on the spot.
   C. By telephone inquiry.
   D. By face-to-face interview.
2. According to the passage, what serious negative consequences may compulsive buying cause?
   A. Financial crisis, unhappy marriage, unemployment and even suicide attempts.
   B. Pathological gambling and binge eating.
   C. Financial crisis, unhappy marriage, unemployment and even crime attempts.

D. Financial problem, family problem and moral problem.

3. The word "binge" (Line 5, Para. 6) is closest in meaning to the following expressions EXCEPT "_____".

A. uncontrolled   B. excessive

C. negative   D. addictive

4. It can be inferred from the passage that _____.

A. compulsive buyers commonly buy things to improve their mood

B. compulsive buying is a serious recognized psychiatric illness

C. the compulsive buying has already been included in the next edition of the Diagnostic and Statistical Manual of Mental Disorders

D. the survey shows that financially destructive behavior should receive enough attention

5. Where does the passage probably come from?

A. Newspaper.   B. Magazine.

C. Column.   D. Periodical.

II. Decide whether each of the following statements is true or false. Put "T" for true and "F" for false in the space provided.

_____1. Compulsive buying is an abnormal spending behavior.

_____2. It has been generally acknowledged that compulsive buying is one type of psychiatric diagnoses.

_____3. As researchers expected, men and women are equally or nearly equally likely to suffer from compulsive buying.

_____4. Not only do the compulsive buyers suffer from addictive shopping, but also from other psychiatric disorders.

_____5. At present, no psychotherapy or medication is available to help compulsive buyers to stop.

Global Heart Disease Risks

As the prevalence of heart disease increases worldwide, researchers have found that people in developing countries suffer from it for the same reason as people in industrial nations do. Smoking, fatty diets, and stress top the list of heart attack risks.   1

Heart disease is the largest cause of death worldwide. Eighty percent of the cases occur in developing nations, but most of what we know about the causes comes from studies among the people in Western countries, mainly those middle aged white men.   2

Now a new study about 30,000 men and women in 52 nations on every inhabited continent shows that the rest of the world is of no difference. "The factors that cause heart attacks are the same," says Sonia Anand, a physician at McMaster University (麦克马斯达大学) in Hamilton (汉密尔顿市), Ontario (安大略省), Canada. "What we found is nine simply measured risk factors that predict the majority of heart attacks around the world."   3

The researchers say these risk factors account for 90 percent of heart attacks internationally and are consistent across all regions and ethnic groups, young or old, male or female. Of them, two factors stand out, smoking and fatty diets. Together they account for two-thirds of heart attack risks.   4

"There are two most important things that we can do as a society, one is to prevent smoking or encourage smokers to stop, and the second is that we can see the adverse consequences of obesity," says Dr. Anand.

5

Surprisingly that the international study found the third most important cause of heart disease is emotional stress. "Some people think, well, you are stressed out so you are going to eat more or smoke more, and that is why you get your heart attack," she notes. Other but lesser risk factors for heart attack are high blood pressure and diabetes (糖尿病), whereas genetic inheritance (遗传) seems to account for only a tiny portion of this disease, but one percent.

6

Protecting against heart disease is consumption of fruits and vegetables, moderate amounts of alcohol, and regular physical exercises.

7

While industrial countries have enjoyed a decline in heart disease in the past few decades, death rates have increased dramatically in low and middle income nations. Dr. Anand says the findings can help governments determine how to counter the trend.

8

"There is a prediction that countries like India and China will experience an epidemic heart disease by the year 2020," she adds. "These studies allow those countries now to begin to put in place prevention policies to try and cure the epidemic."

9

(443 words)

How fast do you read?

443 words ÷ _____ minutes = _____ wpm

Exercises for Passage 4

I. Choose the best answer for each of the following items in accordance with the passage.

1. Among the factors leading to heart attack, _____ top the list.
   A. smoking, blood pressure and diabetes
   B. smoking, fatty diets and stress
   C. stress, blood pressure and fatty diet
   D. smoking, diabetes and fatty diet.

2. According to the passage, which of the following diseases is the main cause of death worldwide?
   A. Cancer.   B. Smoking.
   C. Heart disease.   D. Weight gain.

3. "Obesity" (Line 3, Para. 5) means "_____".
   A. eating   B. sleeping
   C. drinking   D. weight gain

4. According to the passage, which of the following is true?
   A. Smoking, fatty diets and stress lead to global heart disease risks.
   B. Industrial countries have undergone an increase in heart disease in the past few decades.
   C. High blood pressure and diabetes (糖尿病) seem to account for only a tiny portion of heart disease.
   D. When people are relaxed, they are going to eat more or smoke more and that is why they get their heart attacks.

5. According to the author, besides regular physical exercises, _____.
   A. consumption of fruits and vegetables, drinking large amounts of alcohol can protect against heart disease
   B. consumption of fruits and vegetables, not extreme amounts of alcohol can protect against heart disease

C. consumption of less fruits and vegetables, drinking small amounts of alcohol can protect against heart disease

D. consumption of too many fruits and vegetables, drinking no alcohol can protect against heart disease

II. Translate the following sentences from the passage into Chinese.

1. Smoking, fatty diets, and stress top the list of heart attack risks.

   _____

   _____

2. Other but lesser risk factors for heart attack are high blood pressure and diabetes, whereas genetic inheritance seems to account for only a tiny portion of this disease, but one percent.

   _____

   _____

3. Protecting against heart disease is consumption of fruits and vegetables, moderate amounts of alcohol, and regular physical exercises.

   _____

   _____

Unit 8

Science and Technology

Science is but an image of the truth.

—*Francis Bacon*

Passage 1

Pluto Isn't What It Used to Be

Throw away the place mats. Redraw the classroom charts. Take a   1
pair of scissors to the solar system mobile.

After years of arguing and a week of debate, astronomers voted   2
for a sweeping reclassification of the solar system. In what many

of them described as a victory of science over sentiment, Pluto(冥王星) was degraded to the status of a "dwarf planet."

In the new solar system as defined by the International Astronomical Union meeting in Prague (布拉格，捷克首都), there are eight planets instead of nine, at least three dwarf planets and tens of thousands of so-called smaller solar system bodies, like comets (彗星) and most asteroids (小行星).

3

For now, the other dwarf planets are Ceres, the largest asteroid, and an object known as 2003 UB 313, nicknamed Xena, that is larger than Pluto and, like it, orbits beyond Neptune (海王星) in a zone of icy debris known as the Kuiper Belt. But there are dozens more potential dwarf planets known in that zone, planetary scientists say, and so the number in the category could quickly swell.

4

In a nod to Pluto's fans, the astronomers declared it to be the prototype for a new category of such "trans-Neptunian" objects, but refused in a close vote to approve the name "plutonians" for them.

5

The outcome completed a stunning turnaround from only a week ago, when the assembled astronomers were presented a proposal that would have increased the number of planets in the solar system to 12, retaining Pluto and adding Ceres, Xena and even Pluto's moon Charon.

6

It had long been clear that Pluto, discovered in 1930, stood apart from the previously discovered planets. Not only is it much smaller—only about 1,600 miles in diameter, smaller than the Moon—but its long and narrow orbit is tilted with respect to the other planets,

7

and it goes inside the orbit of Neptune on part of its 248-year journey around the Sun.

Pluto, some astronomers had argued, made a better match with the other ice balls that have since been discovered in the dark realms beyond Neptune. In 2000, when the Rose Center for Earth and Space opened at the American Museum of Natural History, Pluto was denoted in a display as a Kuiper Belt object and not a planet.

8

Under the new rules, a planet must meet three criteria: it must orbit the Sun, it must be big enough for gravity to squash it into a round ball, and it must have cleared other things out of the way in its orbital neighborhood. The last of these criteria knocks out Pluto and Xena, which orbit among the icy wrecks of the Kuiper Belt, and Ceres, which is in the asteroid belt. Dwarf planets, on the other hand, need only orbit the Sun and be round.

9

(463 words)

How fast do you read?

463 words ÷ _____ minutes = _____ wpm

Exercises for Passage 1

I. Choose the best answer for each of the following items in accordance with the passage.

1. The number of potential dwarf planets in the icy wrecks of Kuiper Belt, as pointed out by planetary scientists is to _____.

A. increase   B. decrease

C. reduce   D. fall

2. As far as Pluto's characteristics are concerned, which of the following description is NOT true?

   A. Pluto is rather small compared with the other discovered planets.

   B. The orbit of Pluto is not inclined at all.

   C. The total time for Pluto to travel around the sun is 248 years.

   D. Sometimes Pluto would go inside the orbit of Neptune.

3. The phrase "knocks out" (Line 4, Para. 9) probably means "_____".

   A. leaves out   B. leaves off

   C. leaves alone   D. leaves behind

4. Why is Pluto not qualified to be called a planet according to the new rules?

   A. Because it doesn't orbit the sun.

   B. Because it isn't big or round enough.

   C. Because it has some other heavenly bodies blocked in its orbital neighborhood.

   D. Because it doesn't orbit among the icy wrecks of the Kuiper Belt.

5. It can be inferred from the passage that _____.

   A. Pluto's fans were satisfied with reclassification of Pluto

   B. the debate over the reclassification of solar system was heated

   C. more than 90 percent of voters in Prague meeting voted to disapprove of the name "plutoninans" for those dwarf planets

   D. it was not until recent years that scientists discovered the differences between Pluto and the former discovered planets

II. Decide whether each of the following statements is true or false. Put "T" for true and "F" for false in the space provided.

_____1. There are nine planets in the old-defined solar system.

_____2. The reason why Pluto, Ceres and Xena are defined as dwarf planets is that they are too small.

_____3. Pluto is nearer than Neptune to the sun.

_____4. Both Ceres and Xena which orbit among the icy debris are known as Kuiper Belt.

_____5. To make Pluto's fans feel better, the astronomers declared Pluto to be the example type of such new category heavenly objects as "trans-Neptunian".

Web Surfing in Public Places

Any business traveler who has logged on to a wireless network at the airport, printed a document at a hotel business center or checked e-mail messages at a public terminal has probably wondered, at least fleetingly, "Is this safe?"　　1

Although worrying about computer security is a bit like worrying about a toddler—potential dangers lurk everywhere and you can drive yourself crazy trying to avoid them—the fact is, business travelers take certain risks with the things they do on most trips.　　2

Wireless networks at airports, hotels or cafes are not as secure as most people think. Someone may have some software on their computer that allows them to look at all the wireless transactions going on around them and capture packets that are floating between the laptop and the wireless access point.　　3

These software programs are called packet sniffers and many can   4
be downloaded free online. They are typically set up to capture
passwords, credit card numbers and bank account information—
which is why we say shopping on the Web is not a great way to kill
time during a flight delay.

Using a public computer can also mean courting trouble, because   5
data viewed while surfing the Web, printing a document or opening
an email attachment is generally stored on the computer—
meaning it could be accessible to the next person who sits down.
To remove traces of your work, delete any documents you have
viewed, clear the browser cache and the history file and empty the
trash before you walk away.

Another risk you may also run is that somebody has loaded a   6
program on there that can capture your log-ins and passwords.

One way to foil these programs, which record what you type and   7
can send the transcript to a hacker, is to use a password manager
like RoboForm. This $30 software encrypts all your user's names
and passwords for various Web sites, then enters the data at the
click of a mouse when you are prompted to log in.

There are also simple measures you can take to protect your   8
hardware, like using a cable lock to secure your laptop in a hotel
room or even a cafe (in case you leave the table for any reason),
and making sure you lock your computer bag in the trunk rather
than leaving it on the back seat.

For travelers who do carry around sensitive data, it is worth   9
looking into programs like Absolute Software's LoJack for Laptops,

which can help recover a missing computer. The software reports its location when connected to the Internet—and some versions can even be programmed to destroy data if a computer is reported lost or stolen.

But perhaps the most common snoop that business travelers encounter is someone nearby "shoulder surfing" to see what is on a laptop, out of curiosity or mere boredom.   10

To foil prying eyes, 3M sells a Notebook Privacy Filter, a plastic film that makes it impossible to view a laptop screen from an angle.   11

(498 words)

How fast do you read?
    498 words ÷ _____ minutes = _____ wpm

Exercises for Passage 2

I. Decide whether each of the following statements is true or false. Put "T" for true and "F" for false in the space provided.

_____1. Most people take it for granted that it's safe to surf web in public places.

_____2. In the author's view it seems impossible to completely avoid potential computer security problem.

_____3. By "courting trouble" (Line 1, Para. 5) the author means using a public computer can also invite something disagreeable.

_____4. The most serious problem of computer security comes from "shoulder surfing".

113

_____5. The author holds a negative attitude towards preventing computer security problem.

II. Translate the following sentences from the passage into Chinese.

1. They are typically set up to capture passwords, credit card numbers and bank account information—which is why we say shopping on the Web is not a great way to kill time during a flight delay.

_____

_____

2. To remove traces of your work, delete any document you have viewed, clear the browser cache and the history file and empty the trash before you walk away.

_____

_____

3. The software reports its location when connected to the Internet—and some versions can even be programmed to destroy data if a computer is reported lost or stolen.

_____

_____

$\mathcal{P}$assage 3

Heat May Be Nature's Deadliest Killer

Extremely hot weather is common in many parts of the world. Although hot weather just makes most people hot, it can cause

1

medical problems—and death.

Health experts say that between 1979 and 1999, extremely hot weather killed more than eight thousand people in the United States. In that period, more Americans died from extreme heat than from severe storms, lightning, floods and earthquakes together.

2

The most common medical problem caused by hot weather is heat stress. For most people, the only result of heat stress is muscle pain. If heat stress is not treated, it can lead to a more serious problem called heat exhaustion. A person suffering from heat exhaustion feels weak and extremely tired. Heat exhaustion also may produce a general feeling of sickness, a fast heartbeat, breathing problems, and pain in the head, chest or stomach. Also it can lead to heat stroke. This is the most common cause of death linked to hot weather.

3

Immediate medical help is necessary for someone with heat stroke. Immediate treatment should begin by moving the victim out of the sun. Raise the person's feet up about thirty centimeters. Then, take off the person's clothing. Put water on the body. And place pieces of ice in areas where blood passageways are close to the skin. These areas include the back of the neck and under the arms.

4

Drinking water is very important for cooling the body on hot days. Water carries body heat to the surface of the skin. The heat is lost through perspiration (汗水). Perspiration is one of the body's defenses against heat. However, a person suffering from heat exhaustion loses too much water through perspiration, the person becomes dehydrated (脱水). Dehydration limits a person's ability

5

to work and think. When body temperature is higher than forty-two degrees Celsius (摄氏), permanent brain damage and death may result.

Health experts say adults should drink about two liters of water each day to replace all the body water lost in liquid wastes and perspiration. And in hot weather, people should drink more than that.   6

In hot weather, drinking cold liquids is best because they can help cool us faster than warm liquids. Yet experts say that sweet drinks，tea and coffee are not good to drink in hot weather. Doctors also warn against alcoholic drinks. Alcohol speeds the loss of body water through liquid wastes.   7

In addition to drinking cool water, doctors say there are other things that can protect against the health dangers of heat. Stay out of the sun. Wear loose, lightweight and light-colored clothes. Wear a hat or other head cover while in the sun. Eat fewer hot and heavy foods. Also, rest more often because physical activity produces body heat.   8

These simple steps can prevent the dangerous health problems linked to heat. They will prevent sickness, help you feel better and may even save your life.   9

(476 words)

How fast do you read?

476 words ÷ _____ minutes = _____wpm

Exercises for Passage 3

I. Decide whether each of the following statements is true or false. Put "T" for true and "F" for false in the space provided.

_____1. Between 1979 and 1999, more Americans died from extreme heat than from severe storms, lightning, floods and earthquakes together.

_____2. Heat exhaustion can lead to general feeling of sickness which is the most common cause of death linked to hot weather.

_____3. Immediate medical help for someone with heat stroke is to send him or her to hospital.

_____4. When body temperature is higher than forty-two degrees centigrade, permanent brain damage and death may result.

_____5. Drinking cold liquids is the only way to help cool us down.

II. Translate the following sentences from the passage into Chinese.

1. And place pieces of ice in areas where blood passageways are close to the skin. These areas include the back of the neck and under the arms.

_____

_____

2. However, a person suffering from heat exhaustion loses too much water through perspiration, the person becomes dehydrated (脱水).

_____

_____

3. These simple steps can prevent the dangerous health problems linked to heat. They will prevent sickness, help you feel better and may even save your life.

_____

_____

117

How the Science of the Very Small Is Getting Very Big

One of the most important research fields in technology is called nanotechnology. It is the science of making things unimaginably small. Nanotechnology gets its name from a measure of distance. A nanometer (十亿分之一米，毫微米，纳米) or nano, is one-thousand-millionth of a meter. This is about the size of atoms and molecules. Many experts credit the idea to physicist Richard Feynman, the Nobel Prize winner, he discussed the theory that scientists could make devices smaller and smaller—all the way down to the atomic level.

Two researchers, working for IBM invented what they called a scanning tunneling microscope. This permitted scientists to observe molecules and even atoms in greater detail than ever before. By the middle of 1980's, scientists had increased their research on carbon. They wanted to create nano-structures from carbon atoms. They aimed a laser at carbon. This powerful light caused some of the carbon to become a gas. The scientists cooled the gas to an extremely low temperature. Then they looked at the carbon material that remained. They found, among several kinds of carbon, a molecule of sixty atoms—carbon sixty. Carbon sixty is a group of tightly connected carbon atoms that

1

2

forms a ball. It is a very strong structure.

The next nano-structure development came in 1993, Japanese   3
scientist developed carbon nanotubes. They are extremely strong.
Scientists believe that someday nanotubes could replace the
carbon graphite (石墨) now used to make airplane parts. Soon
after this discovery, researchers started to think about using
nanotubes to build extremely small devices. In 2003, IBM
announced that it had made the world's smallest light.

Nanotubes appear to have many different uses. For example, to   4
make a flat material, or film, out of nanotubes. The film is about
one-thousandth the width of human hair. Scientists believed it
could be used to make car windows that can receive radio signals,
to make solar electricity cells light or thin, moveable displays that
show pictures like a television. Computer scientists hope
developments in nanotechnology will help to break barriers of size
and speed. In 2003, IBM announced that it had created the
world's smallest transistor based on the element silicon (硅元素),
which was four to eight nanometers' thick.

Although nanotechnology is exciting, there are concerns about   5
the safety of super small structures. Scientists and environmental
activists worry that nano-materials could pass into the air and
water causing health problems. There is reason for concern. A
study by NASA researchers found that nano-particles caused
severe lung damage to laboratory mice. Other studies suggest
that nano-particles could suppress the growth of plant roots or
could even harm the human body's ability to fight infection.

The Environmental Protection Agency (EPA) recognizes that   6
there are unknown health risks involved in nanotechnology. And

the government needs to develop rules for nano-materials, which are already being made in hundreds of places around the country.

(473 words)

How fast do you read?
473 words ÷ _____ minutes = _____ wpm

Exercises for Passage 4

I. Choose the best answer for each of the following items in accordance with the passage.

1. According to the passage, which of the following is true?
   A. Nanotechnology gets its name from distance.
   B. A nanometer is one-thousandth of a meter.
   C. The idea of nanotechnology is attributed to a physicist, Richard Feynman.
   D. Nanotechnology is the latest scientific technology.

2. With the help of a scanning tunneling microscope, _____.
   A. scientists could observe more molecules and atoms
   B. scientists could observe more molecules and atoms and even atoms in greater detail than ever before
   C. scientists developed nanotechnology
   D. scientists discovered nano-structures from carbon atoms

3. Scientists believe that someday nanotubes could be used to make airplane parts mainly because _____.
   A. nanotubes are extremely strong
   B. the carbon graphite can not be used any more
   C. nanotubes are extremely small

D. scientists want to use new materials

4. The sentence "Computer scientist hope developments in nanotechnology will help break barriers of size and speed" means "_____".

   A. with further research, nanotechnology will make products light and strong

   B. with further research, nanotechnology will make products light but large

   C. with further research, nanotechnology will make products small but light

   D. with further research, nanotechnology will make products light and strong in small size

5. What do scientists and environmental activists worry about?

   A. Nano-materials might pollute the air.

   B. Nanotechnology development would destroy ecological system.

   C. Nano-material could pass into the air and water causing health problem.

   D. Nano-materials could even harm human's ability to fight infection.

II. Answer the following questions with the information you get from the passage.

1. What aroused scientists' interest in developing nanotechnology?

_____

_____

2. Everything is a two-edged sword, so is nanotechnology. Explain this sentence in your own words.

_____

_____

3. What does the title mean?

_____

_____

Key to the Exercises

Unit 1

Passage 1   Story of Mother's Day

I. 1. C   2. D   3. A   4. D   5. C

II. 1. 最早的母亲节要追溯到古希腊为纪念众神之母瑞亚而举行的春季庆典。

2. 为增加节日的气氛，他们常捎带一种叫"省亲蛋糕"的特制蛋糕。

3. 1914 年，伍德罗·威尔逊总统发表官方通告，宣布母亲节为一个全国性的节日，在每年五月的第二个星期日庆祝。

Passage 2   China's Own Valentine's Day

I. 1. F   2. F   3. T   4. F   5. F

II. 1. 在中国的传说中，牛郎和织女每年都会在银河上的鹊桥相会。

2. 然而，不幸的是王母娘娘发现了织女不在天宫，她非常生气，立即派人把织女带回了天宫。

3. 最后王母娘娘发了慈悲，允许牛郎和织女每年的七夕节在银河上相会一次。

Passage 3   "Happy Father's Day, Dad!"

I. 1. C   2. A   3. C   4. D   5. D

II. 1. T   2. F   3. T   4. F   5. T

Passage 4   Traditions of Easter

I. 1. F   2. T   3. F   4. T   5. T

II. 1. commemorates   2. decreed   3. prior to   4. coincide with

5. observance   6. correspond to 7. uproarious   8. converts to

Unit 2

Passage 1   Ancient Olympics

I. 1. C   2. B   3. D   4. A   5. B

II. 1. T   2. T   3. T   4. F   5. T

Passage 2   Mascots Promise a "Friendly" Olympics

I. 1. F   2. F   3. T   4. T   5. T

II. 1. 它们也代表了自然界中海洋、森林、火、大地、天空五大元素，个个
描绘得栩栩如生，反映出中国民间艺术和装饰的深刻影响。

2. 吉祥物成为向公众尤其是小朋友传达奥运精神的工具。

3. 刘指出：吉祥物具有独特的中国民族特色，它们不仅代表了中国不同
民族的不同文化，而且也体现出中国传统哲学中人与动物的和谐关系。

Passage 3   Amsterdam Olympics 1928

I. 1. D   2. C   3. B   4. A   5. D

II. 1. 即使她们穿着黑色的长统袜，她们也绝对是不可以露出膝盖的。

2. 甚至对女体操队员交叉着腿的团体照片，人们也是不能接受的。

3. 当时，女性参加比赛都穿着受限制的运动服。

Passage 4   Olympic Torch and Flame

I. 1. T   2. F   3. F   4. T   5. T

II. 1. symbol   2. extinguished   3. essence   4. elegance

5. culminated   6. privilege   7. participated   8. traits

Unit 3

Passage 1 Cigarette Causes Blindness

I. 1. D   2. A   3. B   4. C   5. C

II. 1. 欧洲的一项研究显示，可能导致失明的一种重要疾患，即与年龄相关性黄斑病变的主要病因有四分之一以上与吸烟有着直接的关系。

2. 化学物质会对全身的血管造成影响，其中一个间接的后果则是它们会逐渐损害眼组织。

3. 烟草中的化学物质会影响视网膜的新陈代谢，致使人的眼睛未老先衰，引起黄斑病变。

Passage 2 Our Nuclear Lifeline

I. 1. A   2. C   3. D   4. A   5. B

II. 1. T   2. T   3. F   4. T   5. T

Passage 3 Dogs Smell Cancer in Patients' Breath

I. 1. A   2. D   3. D   4. C   5. A

II. 1. 普通家犬仅需接受几周的基础训练就能学会准确无误地将肺癌、乳腺癌病人和健康人的呼吸样本区分开来。

2. 考虑到有些肺癌病人在接受试验前可能刚刚抽烟，研究人员调整了试验结果；即便如此，狗检测癌症的准确率仍然很高。

3. 尽管与人脑相比，狗的大脑有更多部分作用于嗅觉，但究竟是什么使狗如此善于辨别气味还不可得知。

Passage 4 Bug Detectives

I. 1. F   2. F   3. T   4. T   5. T

II. 1. 法医学总是采用我们现有的一切科学知识来对付各种犯罪，但也有其自身局限性。

2. 任何动物的尸体对昆虫都有很强的吸引力。在死亡的数十分钟内，首先到现场的是常见的家蝇。它迅速确定尸体是否是产卵的好地方，这样当卵孵化时，它们会有很方便的食物来源。

3. 通过倒推昆虫活动的生物钟，可以发现其死亡时间的重要线索。

Unit 4

Passage 1   Top of the Class

I. 1. D   2. D   3. A   4. B   5. D

II. 1. 答案当然不在于大量投入教育经费。尽管芬兰中小学教育开销稍高于欧洲平均值，但还是低于某些北欧邻国。

2. 尽管芬兰学校里也存在恃强凌弱、吸毒、学生不尊敬老师等现象，但这些问题会尽早解决；旷课现象也较少。

3. 在瑞典和俄罗斯统治期间，阅读芬兰语和用芬兰语写作已成为民族主义的象征，是一件值得骄傲的事。

Passage 2   Internet Plagiarism

I. 1. B   2. B   3. D   4. A   5. C

II. 1. F   2. F   3. T   4. T   5. F

Passage 3   Boys' Struggle with Reading and Writing

I. 1. C   2. D   3. A   4. B   5. B

II. 1. 甚至有人推测明年在全国理科考试中女孩的成绩也许会超过男孩，这就直接导致女孩在大学入学及就业方面领先于男孩。

2. 有人说导致男孩在写作和阅读方面仍然落后于女孩的原因是由于教育的"女性化"。

3. 但是也有一些人争辩说要保证男孩和女孩享受同等的教育，唯一的办法就是把他们隔离起来接受教育。

Passage 4   When Your Child Hates School

I. 1. D   2. B   3. D   4. A   5. C

II. 1. F   2. F   3. T   4. T   5. F

Unit 5

Passage 1   Circus Animal

I. 1. A   2. C   3. A   4. B   5. A

II. 1. 马戏团本是一个让人开心的地方，孩子们喜欢去那儿。但一旦牵涉到动物，此种快乐却是付出了沉重的代价。

2. 它们被迫生活、游历于远远小于它们野外栖息地的拥挤城区，而不是在自然栖息地自由自在地漫游，依其天性生活。

3. 很多马戏团根本不考虑气候因素，动物们常常暴露在极度炎热或寒冷的条件下。

Passage 2   A Hero and an Angel
I. 1. D   2. B   3. D   4. B   5. C
II. 1. T   2. T   3. T   4. F   5. F

Passage 3   A True Treasure
I. 1. With ropes, bits, bats and spurs, the author dominated them and made them do what she wanted.

2. Failed with the manipulative methods in controlling her horse, and fearing of getting herself killed by this fiery horse, the author began to turn to new ways for help.

3. It is a method of training that focuses on communication.

4. To put it simply, positive effects snowballed on a daily basis. Specifically, her husband became happier and more helpful; her children more actively responsive, polite and considerate. Treasure, her horse has become a perfect horse; and she herself is becoming a role model and be adored by the ones she loves.

5. Every day, the beneficial effect gets rapidly increased.

II. 1. T   2. F   3. T   4. T   5. T

Passage 4   The Cars in Dog Heaven Have No Wheels
I. 1. T   2. F   3. T   4. F   5.T

II. 1.Buford would sometimes scramble up, to stand and drool amid the few large, lopped-off branches before skittering down to wave his long feathery tail at us as we cheered.

2. Buford often carried the kitten around in his mouth—the little thing lying luxuriously across the dog's bottom jaw; then he'd stop and flip it gently

into the air and catch it again. The kitten, dizzy as it got, seemed to love it. Then Buford would set it down, amazingly gently for such a big dog. Once back on land, the kitten would dance drunkenly for a moment before pressing up against Buford's leg in affection.

3. Buford was died of car-chasing, but I think he was still going on to continue his habit in hell where there would be no cars, no danger.

Unit 6

Passage 1   Don't Be Afraid of Worry

I. 1. D   2. A   3. B   4. D   5. B

II. 1. T   2. T   3. T   4. F   5. T

Passage 2   Forgive

I. 1. F   2. T   3. T   4. F   5. T

II. 1. Her mother was abusive and had very little patience and if she made a mistake or caused an accident she would strike her. In addition, her mother was constantly calling her stupid, an idiot, etc. Her father was more interested in her brother, she didn't seem to matter to her father and was pretty much ignored.

2. She tried not to criticize her children harshly, granted her children a lot of freedom and never physically hit her children or damaged their egos by calling them names.

3. She began to feel that her mother had a very difficult life and did not intentionally hurt her.

Passage 3   Grandfather's Lunch

I. 1. B   2. C   3. A   4. D   5. C

II. 1. In wartime.

2. For fear that the food turned cold and thus his grandfather, who liked his lunch served hot, refused to give him any award.

3. They were ready to sit things out until the shooting was over.

4. Run in a zigzag across the road, keeping dodging the bullets.

5. It's impossible to go through life without trials and struggles being thrown at you.

Passage 4　Facing the Challenge

I. 1. B　　　　2. C　　　　3. D　　　　4. B　　　　5. A

II. 1. 我抹去眼泪，抑制住哽咽，拿起听筒。

2. 这时我感觉自己就像是一位被人追寻的骑士，他身穿闪光盔甲，正去救援处于危难中的女士和小孩。

3. 凛冽的寒风吹打着我的脸，大雨倾盆，电闪雷鸣。

4. 我想说"不"，但是我知道，如果我拒绝了，我也许就不会再搭上另一辆三轮车了。

Unit 7

Passage 1　Unable to Fall Asleep Though Tired

I. 1. C　　　　2. D　　　　3. B　　　　4. B　　　　5. A

II. 1. 身体上感到"劳累"却仍然无法入睡是可能的，因为你的身体可能感到疲惫，但你不觉得困倦。

2. 缺少睡眠使事情变得更为复杂。

3. 这样就形成了一个恶性循环：你感觉越来越累，但你的身体受到的刺激却越来越强。周末"强制性睡眠"只是暂时的解决办法。

Passage 2　Yoga

I. 1. C　　　　2. D　　　　3. C　　　　4. D　　　　5. D

II. 1. Since the modern society is anything but peaceful, more and more people have been turning to yoga as a way to ease the troubles of modern life and find peace of mind.

2. Scholars hold that modern yoga dates back to more than 5,000 years ago in the Indus Valley.

3. Yes, they were the holy men of early human civilization, and their role in society was to communicate with the spirit world to find keys to problems

facing their people.

4. It was not until the 1960s when popular culture began to show an interest in Eastern religions that yoga was practically known to the West.

Passage 3   Compulsive Buying

I. 1. C   2. A   3. C   4. D   5. A

II. 1. T   2. F   3. F   4. T   5. F

Passage 4   Global Heart Disease Risks

I. 1. B   2. C   3. D   4. A   5. B

II. 1. 吸烟、高脂肪饮食和压力位于导致心脏病病因的前三位。

2. 高血压、糖尿病是导致心脏病的次要因素，而遗传病似乎只占此病的一小部分，占 1%。

3. 预防心脏病的良方就是摄入一定量的水果和蔬菜，适度饮酒并进行有规律的体育锻炼。

Unit 8

Passage 1   Pluto Isn't What It Used to Be

I. 1. A   2. B   3. A   4. C   5. B

II. 1. T   2. F   3. F   4. F   5. T

Passage 2   Web Surfing in Public Places

I. 1. T   2. T   3. T   4. F   5. F

II. 1. 这些程序主要用来捕获口令、信用卡账号、银行账户信息；这也解释了为什么说航班延误期间进行网上购物并非明智之举。

2. 为了不留下工作痕迹，你在离开之前要删除所有已看过的文件，清除浏览记录和历史文件夹，以及清空回收站。

3. 一旦丢失的电脑接上互联网，该软件就可以找到其位置。有些版本通过编程甚至可以在电脑申明遗失或被盗之后毁坏数据。

Passage 3   Heat May Be Nature's Deadliest Killer

I. 1. T   2. F   3. F   4. F   5. F

II. 1. 并且在血管集中的皮肤表面放一些冰块,这些地方包括脖子的后部及腋下。

2. 然而一个因热虚脱的人会因为出汗失去过多的水分,身体出现脱水症状。

3. 这些简单的方法可以避免和热有关的危险病症,可以使你避免生病,有助于你的健康,甚至可以拯救你的生命。

Passage 4   How the Science of the Very Small Is Getting Very Big

I. 1. C   2. B   3. A   4. D   5. C

II. 1. Making things unimaginably small.

2. Although nanotechnology is of many uses to our society, it may also bring about harmful effects to our environment.

3. The structure of nanotechnology is very small, but its uses may be innumerable in the future.